APACHE BUTTE

The killing and ravaging of Loco and his Apaches would continue until Ken Driscoll could find the men who were supplying them with contraband whiskey. Outnumbered by Indians and renegade whites, further burdened by the necessity of having to find legal proof, Ken knew that his chances of succeeding were about a thousand to one and his chances of surviving about a million to one . . .

GORDON D. SHIRREFFS

APACHE
BUTTE

Complete and Unabridged

LINFORD
Leicester

First Linford Edition
published July 1989

British Library CIP Data

Shirreffs, Gordon D. (Gordon Donald)
Apache Butte.—Large print ed.—
Linford western library
I. Title
813′.54[F]

ISBN 0-7089-6719-1

Published by
F. A. Thorpe (Publishing) Ltd.
Anstey, Leicestershire
Set by Rowland Phototypesetting Ltd.
Bury St. Edmunds, Suffolk
Printed and bound in Great Britain by
T. J. Press (Padstow) Ltd., Padstow, Cornwall

1

CHAIN LIGHTNING lanced through the thick darkness and seemed to plunge into the towering butte to extinguish itself. The lone horseman turned in his saddle, and as he did so the lightning darted through the skies again, illuminating his lean face beneath the hat brim. There was almost something animal-like in the way he tested the night with his senses.

Ken Driscoll's strong hands rested easily on the heavy repeating carbine which lay across his thighs. There was an appearance of power about the man.

Thunder pealed in the canyons and the first great drops of rain struck the harsh earth. Ken pulled his poncho free from the cantle straps, took off his hat, then dropped the poncho over his wide shoulders. For a moment he let the breeze dry the sweat on his forehead and hair, then he replaced his hat on his head, but the interval had been long enough for the flickering light to reveal the etched scar which began at the corner of his left eye and ended at the notched lobe of his left ear, giving him a curious, saturnine expression.

Now and then he glanced up at the towering butte to the southeast. It dominated the barren landscape like a gigantic, hunched and brooding old Apache shaman. The Bold Butte country was the last place he had wanted to come on his quest, but he had exhausted all other possibilities, hating the thought of coming here, yet somehow knowing he would find that which he sought beneath the towering, haunted butte which had given the country its name.

It was whiskey which had brought him to the Bold Butte country. He sought the source of the whiskey which had been traded to the Apaches for gold and loot. It was the fuel of the fires of hell that drove the braves to pillage, rape and kill. Their raids were not sporadic. It seemed almost as though they ran on a schedule. A raid would slash its way across a part of Arizona Territory for a week or ten days, then the raiders would vanish for two weeks, only to reappear, miles from the scene of their last raid, to raze and defile again.

Ken had heard that Loco was loose in the country south of Bold Butte. Diabolito was raiding along the Verde. Nachee was handling the precinct on both sides of the San Carlos. It was bad enough when one of them was on the raiding path; two were rough enough to have every troop and company out in the field against them; the three of them together held the key to the door of hell.

Every man who had been sent into the Mogollon country to find the source of the contraband whiskey had either given up the search through fear and despair, had died quickly, or had vanished without trace. Army men, Indian Bureau agents, US marshals, sheriff's deputies and even the loyal Apache Scouts.

Someone had thought of Ken Driscoll months before as being the man for the job, but he had refused. His scouting days were part of the past. Ranching had been his game until five months ago. That is, until the Tontos had come to his place on Lost Creek, and found Ken's wife and six-year-old daughter there alone while Ken was hunting strays. Ken had heard the shooting and the diabolical screaming of the drink-crazed bucks from the top of the mesa. He had ridden his sorrel to death down the side of the mesa.

3

He had gained and lost many things that bitter day. He had lost wife and child; the stout log house on the banks of Lost Creek; and all of his stock. He had gained the disfiguring slash along the left side of his face, but more than that, more than anything else, he had gained a deep-seated, hatred for the men who had traded whiskey to the Apaches. It was then he had gone to the army, signed up again as civilian scout, and left Fort McDowell on his long search.

Now he wasn't quite sure where he was. He probed into his memories, trying to fit together the pieces of the gigantic puzzle which was the butte country. There were ways through the maze; natural trails which a man would tend to follow, *if* he didn't know the ways of the Apaches who haunted that country. There were other ways as innocent-appearing as quicksand, where a man could vanish and never be seen again. Then there were the owlhoot trails, used by Mexicans coming north to escape the firing squad, and Americans going south to escape the rope.

To his knowledge there wasn't a jackal or an adobe shack within thirty miles of where he was. The Bold Butte Springs were within a short distance ahead of him but he wouldn't stay here. The Apaches had learned long ago that the "white-eyes" usually followed water courses, and always camped near water; quite the reverse of Apache custom.

He looked up as the lightning crackled swiftly across the streaming skies. The butte stood out starkly in the eerie light. For a moment it almost looked like a giant warning finger.

When the darkness came he looked behind him. The thought struck him how odd it was in such a country that a man could quite easily lose himself from anyone, but the Apaches always seemed to know when a stranger was there—and a stranger was always an enemy to an Apache.

There was only one way to beat them, and that was to act and think like an Apache. Ken Driscoll took a perverse delight in out-Apacheing the Apache. But it was a deadly game with no quarter given or taken, and where an Apache might sometimes get careless because of laziness, or because he had taken too much to drink, Ken Driscoll never did. It had kept him alive during his years of army service as a scout, and it would keep him alive until he found the men who had supplied the rotgut for the Tontos. Curiously enough, as much as he wanted to stamp out raiding Tontos, he wanted even more to find the white men who had supplied the whiskey. Then they would find a man who could be more vicious than a drunken Apache!

He slitted his eyes to peer through the wet darkness. The heavy rain seemed to have exhausted itself, and gradually diminished to a fine, slanting veil which obscured the vision. Now and then the lightning oriented him. It was the butte which was his landmark and it seemed as though he'd never get close enough to it to show progress. If he was seen in the open after the dawn he'd end up like half a dozen others who had never come back from their search for the whiskey runners.

They said that no one lingered near Bold Butte and lived. Ken Driscoll digested the thought. One man was going to stay in the Bold Butte country until he found what he was searching for or died in the attempt. That man was Ken Driscoll.

2

IT wouldn't be long until the watery light of dawn came to the Bold Butte country.

The springs were close now. From time to time he looked up at the heights on either side of him. It was time to find a hideout for the coming day. He'd do his scouting on foot.

Then he began to realize he had bet a little too much on his last hand. He had come too far south to find a good hideout.

Then a faint sound came through the wet, windy darkness. Ken drew in the gelding and then swung up the Winchester, peering through the murk. The sound came again—the faint yapping of a puppy. It was somewhere near the unseen springs up ahead.

There were always dogs around Indian encampments, but only those encampments which were relatively safe from attack. No Apache would be fool enough to take a puppy into the Bold Butte country, nor would he tolerate any animal which would give him away.

Ken dropped lightly from the saddle, threw

7

his poncho back over his shoulders, then led the gelding into a maze of huge, jumbled boulders. He ground-reined it and then padded back toward the trail.

There was a faint suggestion of the false dawn in the sky and the rain had stopped.

The wind was shifting as it always did at dawn.

Ken suddenly realized he was closer to the springs than he had calculated, for he recognized a saw-toothed ridge which dropped transversely from the great lion's-paw feet of Bold Butte. The springs were no more than a mile ahead of him, near the wide-mouthed canyon which debouched into the desert country.

He stood there, passing his tongue across his lips, darting his eyes back and forth, watching for some telltale movement in the darkness.

Then he saw a small dark shape move toward him and in a matter of seconds he was back amongst the rocks with his sights on the dim shape. Then slowly he lowered his Winchester and stared, while his heart thudded against his ribs. It was a little girl, or the vision of one.

"Patsy!" The child's clear voice came to Ken.

She wore a dark, hooded cloak and beneath it he saw the lighter coloring of her dress.

8

"Patsy!" she cried again.

Ken shot a glance at the dark heights. Then she was close. "Little girl," he said softly.

She gasped. Ken moved swiftly. He knelt in front of her. "Don't worry," he whispered, "I won't hurt you."

"Who are you?"

"A friend."

"I'm Kathy Ives."

"Please be quiet, and listen to me. You must not call out again. Who is Patsy?"

"My puppy."

"Where are your parents?"

"Gone to Heaven," she said gravely.

It gave him a turn. Here in the middle of nowhere, in a country as deadly as any country could be, with not a white man living within many miles, this mite had turned up, before dawn, looking for her puppy.

There was no warning and the movement came quickly. Ken drove the girl to one side with his right hand and met the charge of the Apache with his left fist thrust out straight. It met flesh and bone and there was a strangled grunt from the buck. The knife went up too slowly after that surprise blow and Ken's left hand locked itself on the strong wrist of the

9

buck, while his knee came up hard against the flapping buckskin kilt and smashed home into soft flesh. As the buck went down on one knee, Ken ripped his Colt from its sheath, swung it up and down in a vicious chopping motion.

Moccasins slapped against the wet earth. Ken whirled, leaped across the fallen warrior, sheathed his Colt and drew his heavy bowie knife. He hunched his left shoulder to meet the second silent attacker, drove it hard against the buck's face and swung his knife in hard and low, just below the ribs.

A heavy weight suddenly struck his back and shoulders and instinctively he hunched forward and twisted to the right; the third warrior smashed hard against the ground. The buck's knife fanged up toward his groin, but Ken deflected the blade with a knee and paid the price of a little blood as he dropped his full weight down onto the Apache's throat. Something cracked dully. Swiftly, Ken's heavy blade probed up beneath the rib cage and pierced the heart.

He stepped back and turned. There was a red devil in front of his eyes. The whole fight had not lasted more than three or four minutes and in that time there had been little sound.

10

There were no other movements in the soaked brush beyond Ken.

He sheathed his bowie after wiping it on one of the buckskin's kilts.

Warm sweat broke out on his lean body as he dragged them one at a time, into the maze of boulders. The gelding shied and blowed.

The child stared at Ken. "Did they hurt Patsy?" she asked.

The incongruity of the question almost caused him to break out into laughter.

Ken turned quickly. Something brushed against his left boot and he looked down to see a squirming puppy. He scooped it up. "Hello, Patsy," he said. He handed the pup to the little girl.

"Thank you," she said. She held the little wet bundle close to her face and her eyes were alight.

The reaction swept over Ken and he felt weak as water. Then he heard the faint sound from somewhere behind him. A muted chanting sound and he knew damned well it wasn't the dawn wind.

In less than a minute he had snatched up the little girl and her precious bundle under one arm while he gripped his Winchester with the

11

other. He darted into the rock maze and placed her on her feet. "You must be quiet," he hissed.

She nodded.

The wind had shifted. The faint sound of thudding hoofs came to them.

Ken gripped his Winchester. He felt the blood running down his leg into his boot. His blood. His hands were wet and sticky against the Winchester.

He could see between the massed boulders far to his left. A head and shoulders swam dimly into view and there were no mistaking the thick mane of hair bound with a headband of dingy white. One after the other, until twelve of them had passed in silent, deadly procession.

The gelding would not whinny nor snort. Its windpipe had been clamped shut too many times by the hands of its master at such times.

Ken moved a little. The girl crouched against a boulder. She moved a little and the puppy opened its mouth. Ken dropped beside the girl. His right hand gripped the pup by the throat and he could feel the life pulsing through the little squirming body. He tightened his grip. The little hind claws raked futilely against his forearm.

"You're . . ." The girl's voice was cut short as she heard a horse snort beyond the boulders.

The pup jerked in a convulsion. Ken dropped the little limp body.

Kathy stared at him. "You," she said. Ken placed his sticky hand over her mouth and felt her struggle as the puppy had done. Little teeth sank into his hard, calloused palm. The child's eyes stared at Ken with hate.

He raised his head. The warriors had passed. A faint chant drifted back on the wind. *"Hoo . . . hoo . . . hoo . . . ahoo. . . ."*

He released the girl. She mechanically wiped the blood from her pale face.

"I'm sorry," he said.

She did not answer. Her hands touched the pup briefly and then she looked away.

"He would have barked," said Ken helplessly.

She did not move. There seemed to be a vacancy in her dark eyes.

The country was probably thick with Apaches, both afoot and mounted. Ken wiped the sweat from his face. Bad enough he had to stay unseen; he had a young female with him. White females had three fates with the hostiles. If they were too young or too weak to travel they died at once; if they were big enough, they were old enough, and maybe some buck would take them into his wickiup for a life of unadulterated hell under his other squaws; if they were full grown they were violated again and again until they died in agony.

The false dawn etched the savage outline of the butte against the watery sky.

Ken picked up his carbine. He walked to the three stiffening corpses. He found a pair of hip-length, thick-soled, button-toed desert moccasins on one of the bodies which was just about the right size for him. As he stripped them from the thick legs he caught the sour odor of rotgut about the dead buck. The three of them must have been loaded to the nines with whiskey. He took off his own boots, and pulled on the moccasins, tying the thongs just below the knees, then he tied his own boots together and hung them over his pommel.

To hole up, that was his only thought. He had plenty of water in three big canteens, and two belts of ammunition. He had beans and bacon, soldier's fare, and coffee, although there could be no fires. But hardtack and water had kept him alive before and it could do so again. But it was the little girl, who stood between him and life. She had hardly made a motion since he had crushed the life from the puppy. He walked to her and squatted in front of her. "Kathy," he said gently.

There was no recognition in the great eyes.

It was getting lighter. The rain was gone. The air seemed to promise a fine day.

She was such a little thing. He could make out her features more clearly. The great brown eyes. The soft dark hair. The clear complexion. The soft little mouth. The very vacancy in her eyes seemed to drive into him.

He picked her up and carried her to the horse. She sat in the wet McClellan and looked away from the man who had saved her life at the cost of her pup's life. Children have a very different sense of values from adults. The end does not always justify the means.

He picked up his Winchester, checked it, then checked his Colt. He took the reins and led the gelding to the south. There was yet a little time before they would be seen.

3

IN a short time the sun would trip the eastern ranges and flood the butte country with warming light.

There was a dawn freshness to the air but it did not drive the scent of death from Ken Driscoll's nostrils.

The little girl had not spoken a word since the pup had been killed.

Overhead, high in the graying sky, a lone buzzard floated against the dawn wind like a scrap of Satan's cloak.

The gelding raised its head and then whinnied. He was answered by the raucous braying of a mule.

Ken stopped short, the mule brayed again. Then the bittersweet odor of woodsmoke came on the wind.

Ken dropped the reins and walked on, with his carbine held forward in his hands and his eyes probing the brush.

There was a group of buildings squatting on the canyon floor where no buildings should have been. A massive fieldstone and adobe structure dominated the other buildings. A partly finished wall surrounded the little cluster of habitations. From the wide chimney of the central building a wraith of smoke drifted slowly and the odors of frying bacon and boiling coffee mingled with the crisp odor of the smoke.

"Madre del Diablo!" said Ken. "What's this!"

The mule brayed again and a man came from the central building, carrying a long-barreled trap-door Springfield. He looked toward Ken. Then he snapped up the rifle.

"God dammit!" yelled Ken. "Put down that cannon!"

The man slowly lowered the heavy rifle and tilted his head forward. "Is that Kathy?" he called.

"Yes!"

"Praise God!" The man turned and kicked open the bolt-studded door. "It's Kathy!" he yelled.

Ken led the gelding toward the house. He glanced back at the little girl. Her face was as impassive as that of the Sphinx. "I guess you're back home, kid," he said.

There was no answer.

17

The woman was the first to reach the little girl. She was tall, almost as tall as Ken, with smooth dark hair drawn tightly back from her oval face. She hardly glanced at Ken as she reached the girl and took her from the saddle.

"Thanks," she said. "Thanks, Mister . . .?"

"Driscoll . . . Ken Driscoll."

He could have bitten his tongue as he heard the thud of feet against the ground behind him. It was a name which should have been kept to himself, at least until he knew who and what these people were.

The hard metal probed against his kidney and he looked back across his left shoulder into the face of the man who had the trap-door Springfield. *"Gracias,"* said Ken dryly.

The man raised his chin a little. "Where'd you have her?" he asked suspiciously, jerking his head toward the girl.

Ken stared at him, stunned, uncomprehendingly.

The muzzle nudged again, this time a little harder.

"Ask her," spat Ken who was furious about the insinuation behind the question.

By this time three other men, one of which

18

was just a kid, had approached and each of them held a pistol in his hand.

The Springfield-man looked at Kathy. "He hurt you, honey?" he asked.

There was no answer, nor had Ken expected an answer.

The slow flame of rage began to flare up within Ken.

Ken looked past him to the other three, and his eyes seemed as hard as his carbine muzzle. "I found her up the canyon, looking for Patsy, before the dawn. I didn't know where she came from."

The woman turned. "I'm her sister, Lila Ives. Why doesn't she speak?" She narrowed her eyes as she saw the drying blood on Ken's clothing and the strange footgear of an Apache.

"I was near the springs just before dawn, like I said. I heard the yapping of a pup, then this little girl came along calling for Patsy. I told her to be quiet."

"Why?"

Ken slitted his tired eyes. "Apaches," he said quietly.

A grizzled tough-looking man called Morg came forward. "You're a liar! There aren't any

19

Apaches around here and if there were they wouldn't give us any trouble."

Ken looked past him at the big building. "You mean you haven't heard they're up?"

One of the men wet his lips. "Jesus," he said softly.

"Where'd you hear about them being up?" asked the man with the Springfield.

"Back on the San Rafael."

"That's a helluva long ways from here."

Ken grinned and looked down at his filthy clothing. "You're not telling me, mister."

The man turned. "Slim," he said, "how far is the San Rafael from here?"

"Fifty mile maybe, Jonce."

Jonce shifted a little. "If you knew they was up, why did you come through them mountains?"

Ken was silent.

"Why?" The word cracked like a pistol shot.

Ken rubbed a dirty hand against the etched scar on his face. "Look," he said mildly, "I brought the little girl in. If I hadn't found her she'd be a *day-den* by now."

Jonce leaned his head forward. *"Day-den?"*

"Apache for little girl."

"You speak Apache?"

20

"Some."

"He looks like a damned 'breed," said the filthy Morg.

Ken's hard eyes met Morg's. For a fraction of a second Morg tried to hold that icy stare and then he looked away.

"You keep your mouth shut, Morg," said Jonce.

Morg went white but his jaw tightened and his right hand moved a little on the pistol grip.

"I'll be getting along," said Ken.

None of the men moved but Ken knew sure as fate that they weren't through with him yet. "There were three bucks back there. They must have heard her calling out. *They* won't be around here to bother you, but there are a dozen more somewhere around here. Might be watching us right now."

Jonce walked around behind Ken and took the reins of the horse. "Move," he said quietly.

They all walked toward the big house, and Ken was the only one who did not look behind himself with quick, darting glances.

Niles, the youngest of the men, looked at Ken. "What happened to those first three 'Paches?"

Ken looked down at the black bloodstains on

his clothing. Blood had clotted on the stiff hairs of his right wrist. "Like I said, they won't be around to bother you."

"Real he-coon," said Morg.

"Go back and look, if you've got the guts," said Ken.

"Damn you!"

"Take it easy, Morg," said Jonce. "You got no call to get riled up."

They walked through the wide gateway. Thick, bolt-studded doors leaned against the walls on either side. "What is this place?" asked Ken.

"Bold Butte Ranch," said Jonce.

"Looks like a fort."

"Started out to be a home station for the Southern Arizona stage-line. Company went broke," said Niles, the kid.

"Hand me those guns," said Jonce.

Ken turned a little, then stepped back to face the four of them. Lila Ives took the little girl into the house, glancing back at Ken as she did so. There seemed to be fear, or sympathy in her dark eyes.

Ken felt the old perverseness rise in him. "I brought the girl back," he said. "If it hadn't been for her I'd be well out into the open country by now. We're even up, hombre."

"You don't hear very well."

The kid was the only one of them who seemed partial to Ken. "Let him go," he said.

Jonce cut the young man short with a wave of his thick hand. "Quiet! This hombre comes riding out of nowhere with my niece and gives us a damned bull story about Apaches."

"It's true," said Ken.

Morg spat. "We'll decide about that."

Jonce reached for the Winchester. Ken turned and as he did so Morg snatched a wagon spoke from the ground and threw it with all his strength. The end struck Ken flush on the forehead and he staggered back, dropping the Winchester. Jonce kicked at him and as Ken went down on one knee the rancher snatched Ken's Colt from the holster.

Jonce, Slim and Morg moved in but something happened so swiftly they jumped back in alarm. Ken came up off the ground and as he did so his right hand swept behind him and reappeared with a thick-bladed bowie in it, cutting edge up.

Morg raised his pistol.

"No!" said the kid.

Jonce shoved back his hat. "Put away the *cuchillo*, Driscoll," he said.

Ken backed off. There was little chance of him breaking away from them, and he was damned if he'd leave the place without his weapons.

They stood about him in a semicircle and all they could do with their weapons was to keep him at bay.

"Put away the knife," said Jonce. His blue eyes had an icy look. "If your story is true nothing will happen to you."

"What do you want me to do?" asked Ken. "Bring in witnesses?"

Morg rushed him. The knife flicked out and traced a red line down the man's left forearm. Morg cursed. He stepped back from the shifting, weaving knife.

Something smashed down on Ken's head and as he went down on his knees he saw Morg's uplifted boot. As Ken came back to consciousness, he got to his hands and knees. His eyes slowly focused in the distance behind the men.

"Look," whispered Ken from his smashed mouth.

Four pairs of eyes followed his gesture.

"Brush fire," said Slim.

24

"After *that* rain?" said Jonce.

"Don't mean a damned thing," said Morg.

The kid stared in rapt fascination and muttered "Mebbe so."

Suddenly, as though formed from the wetness of the granite rock, something began to flash from the butte.

"Mirror signals," said Ken. *"Now do you believe me?"* His head fell forward and he passed out again.

4

THE cool wet cloth passed across his face again and he opened his eyes. It was Lila Ives looking down at him. "Thank God," she said quietly.

Ken moved his eyes. His body ached all over and his mouth was salty. He lay on a bunk in a small room with a beamed ceiling. A shaft of sunlight came in through a narrow loophole, and dust motes danced in the light. From somewhere outside he heard the thudding of a hammer on wood.

She placed the cloth on his forehead and then stood up. Ken threw the cloth to one side and sat up. "Where is he?" he demanded.

"Who?"

"Morg, or whatever his name is."

"Morgan Vestel."

She placed a hand on his shoulder and pressed him back on the bunk. She was surprisingly strong. "You're in no condition to challenge him, Mister Driscoll."

26

She was right. Ken would have had a hard time keeping his fists up.

"I want to thank you again for bringing Kathy home," she said.

"Yeh," he said dryly.

"I didn't know what they intended to do."

"Could you have stopped them?"

"I can handle a gun," she said.

"How is she?"

There was a worried look in her great brown eyes. "She hasn't spoken yet. What happened?"

"I found her first and then the pup found me. The pup came along after the fight."

"Fight?"

"Three Apaches," he said.

"Go on."

"We holed up in the rocks. Twelve more of them came along on horses. The pup would have given us away. I guess I held its throat too hard."

She looked away.

"You believe me, don't you?"

"Of course."

He closed his eyes. Morg had given him a tremendous smash in the face, but Ken's time would come. Ken smiled with anticipation.

"You are a strange man, Mister Driscoll."

27

"No different than any other."

She shook her head. "No. I can tell." She rinsed out the cloth in a basin and placed it on his forehead. "A man rides through Apache-infested country, saves the life of a little girl, gets badly beaten into the bargain and then manages to smile. Why?"

He closed his big hands and looked at them thoughtfully. "Anticipation, ma'am . . . *anticipation*."

"You may have to fight by his side, Mister Driscoll. There have been smoke signals on the butte most of the morning. We haven't seen any of the Apaches but there must be quite a few of them."

Jonce Ives came to the door. "I'm sorry for this mess, Driscoll," he said.

"You didn't do much to stop it, mister."

Ives wet his lips. "Morg Vestel is a rough man."

Ken looked at him through narrowed eyes. "Who's the boss around here?"

"I am."

Ken took the cloth from his head and tossed it onto the table. "I'm sorry there is a lady present, Ives. I'd like to tell you what I think of you and your pack."

28

Ives flushed. "This is no time to harbor grudges, Driscoll."

Ken felt his battered face. "*Grudges*, he says."

"There are only five of us here at the ranch to fight. Six men, counting you." Ives leaned against the wall. "Unless of course, you want to go out into the desert."

"How far do you think I'd get?"

Ives grinned crookedly.

Lila took the cloth and the basin. "There are soldiers at Fort Ballard."

Ives nodded. He fingered his big nose. "We can't send anyone after them until it gets dark."

Ken sat up and placed his back against the wall. "Likely they've got their hands full as it is. Diabolito is raiding along the Verde. Nachee is taking care of the ranches along the San Carlos. I heard that some of them raided the stage station at Dragoon's Farewell and slaughtered every man and woman there."

Ives smashed a fist into his other palm. "If I only had had a little more time! Time to get the walls done and time to hire more men."

"You could have," said Lila quietly, "but those all-night poker games tired out the men."

29

"Shut up!" he said angrily. "Lucky I give you a home here!"

"With the money I brought, Uncle Jonce."

He flushed. "Get out!"

She left the room with her head held high.

Jonce spat. "High tone, she is. Been that way ever since she got here a month ago, damn her." He studied Ken. "Where you running to?"

Ken eyed him. There was something furtive about the man.

"You hear me?" asked Jonce.

"Yeh."

The man leaned back against the wall. "You kill three 'Paches practically in my back yard. You know what that means?"

"You tell me."

Jonce looked out of the window. "I ain't had no trouble with them since I been here."

"Nice," said Ken softly.

Jonce turned quickly. "I never bother them —they never bother me. Now . . . I don't know."

"Maybe I should have let them have the little girl."

The eyes hardened. "They'll find those three

30

bodies. Then they'll come poking around here. You know what happens then?"

"What?"

Jonce grinned, but there was no mirth in his eyes. "I turn you over to them."

The cold, hard words struck home into Ken like the impact of a flint arrowhead. He opened his mouth and then closed it. A thought had come to him with the same impact of Jonce's words.

Jonce grinned again. "You ain't so talkative now, hombre."

Ken eyed him. "You've got my guns. You've got my life in your hands."

Jonce yawned. "They say an Apache can keep a man alive a long time. Long enough so that even your own mother wouldn't recognize you whilst you still had a little life left in your body."

A coldness came over Ken. The man meant what he was saying. There wasn't any doubt about that.

"You really a 'breed?" asked Jonce.

"No."

"Anyone see you kill them three bucks?"

"The little girl."

"Anyone else? Apaches, maybe?"

Ken grinned crookedly. "You think I'd be here now if they had?"

Jonce rubbed his bristly jaws. "Where'd you learn to speak Apache?"

"Here and there."

"Gabby, ain't you?"

Ken touched the bruises on his face. "Not any more."

Jonce looked out of the window toward the great butte.

"You want me to ride to Fort Ballard for help, Ives?" Ken asked quietly.

The man hardly moved. "You couldn't get through."

"I think I can."

Jonce whirled. "You think crap!"

Ken jerked his head in the general direction of the butte. "They're watching this place right now. You said you needed time to get the walls done and to hire more men. That time is gone. Your only hope is to get a man through to Fort Ballard."

"I let you go and you won't come back!"

Ken grinned. "I'm not that loco."

"But would you go to Ballard?"

"Yes."

Jonce spat. "Crap!" he said. He straightened

32

up and walked to the door. He turned slowly. "You ain't leaving here, hombre," he said in a low voice. "I can use you as a sort of ace in the hole. One way or another, hombre. *One way or another.*" He closed the door behind him.

Ken felt for the makings and rolled a cigarette. He lighted it and watched the smoke drift leisurely toward a loophole. The house was strongly built, with walls two-feet thick. Half a dozen determined men could hold it until hell froze over, given enough water and ammunition. Sure, the Apaches could tear the rest of the place to pieces, but it would be a small price to pay for the lives of the people in the house, especially the two females.

Ken blew a smoke ring. He knew he could get away from the place and into the desert. His chances would be fair, but he wasn't in any mood to stay at Bold Butte Ranch and fight alongside men like Jonce Ives and Morgan Vestel. If it wasn't for the two sisters he wouldn't think twice about it.

Ken got up and looked out of the window. Slim was placing a ladder against the side of the house. He climbed it, trailing a long Sharps rifle. Morgan Vestel was working on the hinges of the gate, while a slim Mexican was lashing water kegs onto a burro.

Ken tried the door. It opened easily and he found himself in a large patio or court, surrounded by the big house, it was littered with wood shavings, partially completed furniture, broken—crates and empty barrels. Ives hadn't been there long from the looks of things.

The little girl was seated in a chair beside a sickly looking potted plant. A tattered rag doll lay beside her feet and Kathy was staring toward the great butte. Ken threw down his cigarette and walked to her. "Hello," he said with a smile.

There was no answer, nor was there a change in her set expression. Ken knelt in front of her and handed her the doll, but her hands fell listlessly to her sides. "I'll find another puppy for you," he said.

It was no use. She turned away.

"How long will this last?" asked Lila from behind him.

He turned. "*Quien sabe?* I saw a woman this way once," he said softly. "It was not too long ago, Lila. The Tontos had caught her when her husband was away. She lived the rest of her life without speaking a word. She did not live long." He placed a hand on her shoulder. "Kathy is young. It was a shock, but she'll pull out of it."

"I hope so."

"She will."

"What if the Apaches come?"

Ken looked away. "There is only one thing to do to her."

"And myself?"

"Yes."

She turned away. "I have placed your guns in your room, Mister Driscoll. I got them from my uncle by promising that you would use them only against the Apaches."

"Thanks," he said dryly.

5

HIS guns lay on the bunk. He checked them, and then sheathed the Colt. For a moment his hands tightened on the Winchester and he glanced through the window to where Morg Vestel was working. But the time wasn't now. Ken had the spidery patience of the Apache. He could wait and savor his revenge to the fullest; that was the Apache way.

He walked across the sunlit patio to the kitchen door, glancing at the little girl, but there was nothing on her pale little face.

The kitchen was deserted. He filled a cup with coffee and carried it into the big common room. A thick bed of ashes was in the fireplace and a tendril of smoke wavered up the wide chimney mouth. The slim Mex was seated at the table, drinking coffee. His liquid eyes flicked toward Ken. "Federico Zaldivar, *servidor de ustedes*," he said politely in the old fashion.

Ken nodded. He still didn't know who had

36

struck him down from behind. He raised a hand and touched the knot at the back of his head.

Zaldivar smiled. "Yes, it was my blow," he said apologetically.

"*Gracias*," said Ken dryly.

The slim brown hands were held out, palms upwards. "He is my *patron*. You understand?"

Ken sat down and placed his Winchester on the table with the muzzle pointing at Federico's lower chest. The dark eyes flicked down and up again. Ken sipped his coffee and studied the Mexican.

Federico smiled. "I am out of coffee," he said.

"Go get some then."

The Mexican smiled again, thinly this time. He hurried toward the kitchen, glancing back as he did so.

"Get back here when you get it," called out Ken.

"*Si!*"

The Mexican came back and sat down, away from that deadly gun muzzle. "You see?" he said brightly. "Senor Ives forgives you. You have your guns, *amigo*."

Ken nodded. "Where's his stock, *hombre?*"

The dark eyes became veiled. "It is in the

37

south. We plan to ride south and bring the herd back within a few weeks."

"So?"

"So."

"With the Apaches up all over this part of the territory?"

"We do not fear . . ." The voice trailed off.

"Fear what, *amigo?*"

Federico recovered swiftly. He slapped his chest. "We are men of men," he said boastfully. *"Muy bravo!"*

Jonce Ives came into the room. "Damn you, Federico!" he snapped. "I ain't paying you to sit here and play the coffee pot! Go git that water!"

The Mexican jumped to his feet and hurried to the door.

Ken finished his coffee.

"You got your guns," said Jonce.

"Thanks."

"Now I don't want any trouble here. You just forget what happened."

"You won't have any trouble. *I won't forget what happened.*"

Ken got up and followed Jonce outside. The Mexican was leading his burro toward the springs. The springs were a good three hundred yards from the house, up a small branch canyon. Ken leaned against the wall and watched Federico. "He's a brave man," said Ken to Ives.

Jonce spat. "*Him?* You make me laugh."

Ken scratched his chin. "Takes guts to go in there alone under the eyes of the Apaches."

Jonce glanced quickly at Ken, opened his mouth and then shut it. He walked toward the walled corral.

The slopes of the canyon seemed barren of life. The wind moved the brush and trees, but there wasn't a sign of life, not even a hawk hanging in the clear sky.

Slim leaned over the parapet of the roof. "Maybe they're gone?" he suggested.

"They're usually around when you can't get a sight or smell of them. I've seen them dig holes out in the open desert, then cover themselves over with blankets and earth, so that you'd swear there was nothing on the desert but dried coyote and rabbit crap. Then, when you get too sure of yourself, they'll come out from underneath those blankets like devils straight from hell!"

Slim leaned on his rifle. "You know a lot about them."

"Enough to keep away from them."

"Then what were you doing coming through the mountains when you knew they were up?"

Ken turned his head and eyed the man and Slim flushed and turned away quickly. "Forget it," he mumbled.

Ken remembered the springs from long ago. There were five shallow rock pans, each one at a lower level than the next one. Below the pans the canyon floor was thick with greenery, through which birds fluttered. It was a pleasant place until you knew you were being watched by unseen eyes.

Ken walked to the gate, past the sweating Vestel. The big man looked at him, then down at the Winchester in the big brown hands. He wiped the sweat from his face. Ken walked outside and looked up and down the canyon. It was a good place. Shelter from winter winds; plenty of good water; grazing beyond the canyon; timber on the lower slopes of the mountains. A man could live well at Bold Butte, *if* he overcame the curse which was said to hover over it.

A man could be a king here. With a *corrida* of good *vaqueros*, a fine herd, and plenty of drive and determination.

40

He looked up the slopes. There was no smoke, no vestige of man or animal, nothing but the huge, towering butte dominating the clear sky.

He looked to the south, down the great canyon, to where the desert shimmered under the hot morning sun. There was a rising thread of dust far out on the wastes. It wasn't a wind-devil. Perhaps a stagecoach or a wagon; perhaps a small party of horsemen. Whoever it was was being watched by the keenest eyes in the world atop Bold Butte.

Federico reappeared, leading the trotting burro. Water dripped from the kegs. Still no sign of the Apaches. It was uncanny.

Just as the Mexican reached the gates, smoke showed at the top of the butte. It was just a sudden puff which rose rapidly like a ball of cotton.

Jonce Ives stood near the corral, whittling a chew of tobacco. "They're still there," he said to Ken.

The men were all outside now, watching the heights.

"What does it mean?" asked the kid.

"Steady smoke like we saw this morning means they want to collect scattered parties

41

here at the butte, with hostile intentions, if practical."

Morgan Vestel spat thickly.

"And what does this one puff mean?" asked Slim from the roof.

"Strange party on desert below. I saw dust out there."

"Look!" said Federico.

Smoke puffed up again, this time in neat, compact balls, a string like widely spaced beads, which floated high over the windless top of the butte.

"And *that*, *amigo?*" asked Federico.

"Travelers. Well armed and numerous."

"Whites?" asked Jonce.

"Yes."

"Know quite a bit, don't you?"

"Enough," said Ken dryly.

Slim stared at him. "Are you a 'breed or not, Driscoll?"

Ken spat. "Yeh. One quarter Oglalla Sioux; one quarter Papago; one quarter Negro; one quarter Chinese. Just don't ask me how my pa and maw got together. It's always been a mystery to me, too."

Slim flushed.

Ken walked toward the house. "Any frontiersman worth his salt could have told you what I just told you."

"The cocky sonafabitch," said Vestel.

"It's a lot more than you know, Morg," said the kid.

"Bull crap!"

Federico grinned as he began to unlash the kegs. "I would like to see you take on Driscoll, even up, Morg. Knives, fists or *pistolas*."

The big man turned. "Maybe you'd like to try?"

Federico's fingers stopped moving and his eyes met those of Vestel. "With the *knife*, *amigo?*" he asked softly.

Jonce stowed his tobacco into his mouth. "Enough!" he said thickly. "We got enough work to do without fighting amongst ourselves."

The door closed behind Ken.

"Where'd he come from, you think?" asked the kid.

"Like the wind," said the Mexican. "From nowhere to nowhere."

"The bastard is a 'breed," said Vestel.

"He brought the kid back," said Jonce.

"Yeh," snapped Vestel. "And you fell for it!

The kid can't talk, can she? Can she say what was done to her?"

"What do you mean, Morg?" asked the kid.

Morg glanced toward the house. "He comes out'a nowhere with the kid. The kid ain't hurt in her body, but she can't talk! So Driscoll gets welcomed here like a guest."

"Some welcome," said Federico dryly.

"Shut your gab!" said Morg. He wet his thick lips. "So Driscoll stays here, right in the damned house, and we let him."

"So?" asked Federico.

"We don't know nothing about him. He don't say nothing. Jonce hands him back his guns like a damned idjit. What's to stop him from drygulching all of us, one at a time?"

Federico drew out his knife and ran a thumb along the honed edge. He looked at the house. "You think he suspects anything?" he asked softly.

Jonce shifted his chew and spat. "Wait until Reno gets here," he said.

"Why?" jeered Morgan Vestel. "Can't you make a decision yourself?"

Jonce flushed. He opened his mouth and juice dribbled down his stubbled chin. "Damn you!" he said.

44

Morg grinned. "Or maybe it's your wife what makes the decisions for both you and Reno?"

Jonce dropped his hand to the butt of his Colt, and for a moment his eyes clashed with those of Vestel. The rancher looked away. "We got no call to fight amongst ourselves. Driscoll don't know anything . . . *yet.*"

"And if he finds out?" asked Federico.

Jonce looked at the house. "We can use another man. If Driscoll is all right we can take him in with us. If he ain't . . ."

The three men, Ives, Vestel and Zaldivar looked at the house. The kid walked softly toward the corral.

High overhead, above the great butte, there was a filmy trace of smoke, nothing more.

6

THE fire crackled in the huge fireplace and the light of it flickered on the thick, whitewashed walls, illuminating parts of the large common room, and plunging other parts into semi-darkness.

Jonce Ives sat near the fireplace, with his coffee cup in his thick hands, while he stared into the flames. Slim leaned against the zinc-topped bar which ran along the west wall of the room, relic of the stage station which never was.

Ken Driscoll sat in a chair near the door, watching Lila Ives as she cleared the table of the supper dishes. Overhead he could hear the faint footfalls of the kid as he paced his sentry beat on the roof.

The door opened and Morgan Vestel came in. He leaned his rifle against the wall.

"How is it, Morg?" asked Slim.

"What did you expect!"

Slim flushed. "Nothing."

"That's what's out there . . . nothing." Morg

spat into the fireplace. "Waste of time," he said. He eyed Jonce.

Ken half-closed his eyes. Jonce Ives had set up a sentry schedule, but none of the men seemed to take it seriously. Yet, with the hills as alive with Apaches as a coyote with fleas, they should have been scared aplenty.

"Lila!" said Morg, "give me something to eat."

She served him silently, ignoring his glances at her. He ate noisily, washing down his meat and beans with great gulps of coffee, and all the while he watched her as she walked back and forth. Like a rutting stag, thought Ken.

"You see anything out there?" asked Jonce of Morg.

"I already said I didn't."

"They ought'a be nearing here by now," said the rancher. He quickly eyed Ken, as though something had been let slip.

"Who?" asked Ken. "The Apaches?"

Jonce did not answer.

Ken stood up. "If someone is going for help they'd better leave soon," he said quietly. "The moon will be up before too long."

There was no answer. Ken looked at all of

47

them. Lila paused in the kitchen door and then walked out of sight.

"You willing to go?" asked Morg casually.

"Yes," said Ken.

"Figgered you would."

Lila walked into the room carrying a big coffee pot. She filled the cups and then stopped beside Morg to fill his cup. He dropped his right hand and fumbled about with it. She flushed, jerked her skirts free and dribbled hot coffee on his hairy hand. "Damn you!" he said.

Lila walked back into the kitchen.

Ken stood up and reached for his rifle. He heard the double-clicking of a gun hammer behind him and he slowly turned to see Morg Vestel sitting there with his Colt in his hand, and the muzzle was as steady as Bold Butte. "I thought I'd get out of here while it was still dark," said Ken.

Morg grinned unpleasantly. "Listen to him," he jeered.

Something thudded on the roof and flakes of plaster fell from the ceiling.

"It's the kid," said Slim. "He's seen something."

Jonce walked quickly to the door and opened it.

Ken glanced at the big harp lamp. The light from it would silhouette a man clearly in that wide doorway, and if an Apache buck had a rifle centered on the doorway he could hardly miss. But Jonce was gone, leaving the door open, and Slim was right behind him.

Ken leaned against the wall and watched Morg. Morg stood up, wiped his mouth with the back of his free hand, then gestured toward the door with his Colt. "Go on, 'breed," he said. "Leave the Winchester here."

Ken walked outside. He climbed the ladder and stood on the parapeted roof beside the kid. Jonce, Slim and Federico stood at the southern parapet looking off into the darkness toward the canyon mouth.

Morg came heavily up the ladder and stood behind Ken.

"The wind shifted," said the kid, Niles. "I could have sworn I heard hoofbeats."

"Apaches?" asked Slim.

Ken spat. "If they're out there," he said, "you won't hear them."

"The expert," said Morg.

The wind moaned softly through the wide canyon. The butte was hardly distinguishable in the deep darkness before the coming of the moonlight.

The brush moved uneasily in the cool wind. An owl hooted and a moment later its call was answered by one of its mates.

"Apaches maybe," said the kid.

"No," said Ken. "*Bu*, the owl, is bad luck for them."

He looked up at the butte. It was almost impossible to distinguish its huge outline, but it was there, because it had the faculty of being felt as well as seen.

There was a sharp ringing sound down the canyon. The striking of a shod hoof against a stone.

Something moved in the brush fifty yards from the house.

Ken rested his hand on his Colt.

There was a faint suspicion of moonlight in the eastern sky. The moon would soon be up and then each blade of grass in the canyon would stand out in the cold light.

The wind shifted and blew the smoke down the canyon.

"Hello, the house!" a man called out.

The men on the roof, with the exception of Ken, seemed to relax.

50

"It's Van," said Jonce. "Kid, go on down and tell Lila to make some more food and put on another pot of coffee."

Niles left the roof.

Ken saw the vague outline of a man on a big horse. The horse moved toward the southern gate of the courtyard. "Hey, Jonce!" he called out.

"Yeh, Van?"

"Got a surprise for you."

"So?"

"Reno brought Amy and her maid along with us."

"Christ," said Jonce, as though to himself, "I thought she was in Tucson sitting on her butt."

Morg spat. "Run out'a money, Jonce."

Reno, thought Ken, *Reno* . . .

Van brought his horse into the courtyard. "You know how she is, Jonce," he said loudly.

"Yeh . . . *I know how she is.*"

"Reno didn't mind," said Van. He laughed softly.

Reno. Reno. *Reno*. The name cut through Ken's mind like a lance.

"Who's Reno?" asked Ken of Slim.

51

"Maynard Reno. Trader. Brings stuff in here for Jonce."

Good Christ, thought Ken.

"Let's all go down and greet the weary travelers," said Morg with heavy humor.

Ken looked toward the west parapet. There was a chance for him to drop over into the patio, then get out through the south gate of the enclosure, before Reno saw him. But he had only his Colt and no horse. The odds were too high. As though to settle the matter, Morg jabbed his pistol muzzle against Ken's back. "Down, Rover," he said.

Ken went down the creaking ladder. He could hear more horses down the canyon and the sound of voices. None of them seemed concerned about the Apaches who must be haunting the lower slopes of the butte.

Morg walked into the house while the others stood in the dark courtyard and looked toward the south.

Jonce turned toward Ken. "Where's Morg?" he asked.

"In the house."

"Go on in there with him."

Ken shrugged. He opened the door. Morg was standing by the bar.

"Give me that six-shooter," Morg said.

"Jonce said I was to keep my guns," said Ken evenly.

"Crap! Reno is here now. Jonce takes orders from him, and I know damned well Reno ain't going to let a bastard like you wander around here armed."

Ken drew out his Colt and handed it to the big man. Morg thrust it under his belt, sheathed his own Colt and then walked to the bar. He reached across it, poured a drink and downed it.

Ken still had his knife. He could draw and throw before Morg could turn.

The sound of stamping hoofs, jingling spurs and bits, and loud voices came into the room.

The door swung open and a woman came into the room. She wasn't quite as tall as Lila Ives, but she carried herself in such a fashion that she looked taller than she really was, and the hat she wore heightened the illusion. She wore a fawn-colored riding habit, corded with black, and a gold watch pinned between her full breasts. The firelight shone on her fine blonde hair and glistened from her full moist lips.

Jonce Ives came in behind her. "Amy," he said uncertainly, "I wasn't expecting you."

Ken stared at her. How had Jonce Ives corraled such a filly?

She threw her riding crop onto the table. "This room smells to high heaven," she said. "Lila! Bring me coffee please! *Fresh* coffee. It's been a most tiring ride, Jonce."

"I know, honey," he said solicitously.

She looked at Ken. "Who is the gentleman?" she asked.

Morg grinned.

"Drifter," said Jonce. "Name of Driscoll. Ken Driscoll."

The blue eyes surveyed Ken, and although she made a good portrayal of a woman of breeding and fashion, looking at a stray cur, it seemed to Ken, there was just a little more than just plain curiosity in her look. He eyed her in return.

The faint and delicate odor of jasmine came to him as she moved toward the table and then sat down. *By God, she was a woman!*

Amy Ives looked at Morg. "Call Mister Reno in," she said.

"Yes, ma'am!" Morg raised his filthy hat and walked quickly toward the door. He grinned a little as he passed Jonce.

When the door closed behind Morg, Amy

54

looked at Jonce. "I thought I told you to get rid of him, Jonce," she said coldly.

He shrugged. "Good men are hard to find, Amy," he said apologetically, "and besides that, I didn't know you was coming back so soon this time."

"*Were* coming back, Jonce. Where *is* that girl with the coffee!"

Lila came into the room with a tray, cups and the coffee pot. She nodded to her aunt.

The door swung open again and a tall, broad-shouldered man entered.

"Have some coffee, Maynard," said Amy.

Ken passed a hand across his mouth. It had been a long time since he had faced Maynard Reno.

Reno walked toward the table. Any man could recognize the army stamp on him. He took off his white hat and passed a hand through his dark curly hair. "How are you, Jonce?" he asked.

"Fine, Reno."

"Good! Good! I . . ." His voice trailed off as he saw Ken. "Come out into the light, you."

Ken stepped forward.

Reno dropped his hand to his Colt and drew it partway from the holster.

"I am unarmed," said Ken quietly.

"It's been a long time, Driscoll."

"Maybe not long enough, Reno."

Lila paused in the doorway.

"You know each other?" asked Amy.

The cold blue eyes of Maynard Reno studied Ken. A tic began to move on his left temple and his eyes did not blink.

Then the ex-officer moved so swiftly even Ken had no inkling of what was coming. The heavy barrel of the pistol struck Ken alongside the head, driving him back against a chair. He tried to get at his knife but Reno was too fast. Reno was on him in a mad rage. The last thing Ken heard before he passed out was Reno's high-pitched laughter.

7

KEN opened his eyes and stared at the shadowy ceiling, watching the flickering light reveal the inequalities in the plaster.

His head throbbed like a tom-tom, and his left eye was swollen. He moved a little and felt a raking stitch of pain along his scalp. He explored the area with a shaking hand and felt the matted blood and hair.

A candle guttered in the neck of a bottle. He was in a small room, with a tiny barred window which let in a pale shaft of moonlight.

The salt taste of blood was in his mouth. He raised his head and suddenly his stomach revolted and he spewed vomit across the dirty floor.

He lay still after that, wondering if he could sustain another beating at Bold Butte Ranch and live through it.

Somewhere, deep within him, like the hidden source of the springs at Bold Butte, a tiny spark flickered into life, fanned by the breeze of his hatred, and in the warmth of it he forgot his smashed mouth and lacerated head. His big hands opened and closed spasmodically as he stared at the ceiling. He didn't see the rough plaster and the cobwebs, but rather the contorted face of Maynard Reno, the man who had been cashiered from the United States Army because of Ken Driscoll, and there was cold death in the eyes of the man who lay there.

A key turned in the lock and Lila Ives came into the room, carrying a basin and some soft cloths. "How are you?" she asked in a low voice.

"Look at me."

The room stunk of sweat, blood and vomit. The faint breeze which crept into the room could do little to dissipate the foul odor. There was another, indefinable odor there; the cold aura of death, an effluvium which seemed to emanate from the big man who lay on the bunk.

"Lie still," she said. She wet a cloth and began to bathe his head. "Why did he do it?"

"Where is he?"

"You can't do anything to him now."

He nodded.

"You didn't answer me."

She sat back and studied him. "You have no

one here to take your part beyond me, Mister Driscoll. There isn't one of them out there, with the possible exception of Niles, who wouldn't kill you at the drop of a hat."

"I'll get him," he said thickly. His breath was foul and his eyes were like chips of wet granite.

"Why did he do it?"

He closed his eyes. "It's a long story. Maynard Reno was once an army officer. Even in those days he was a rotten specimen. I was attached to his command as a scout. Three of his men deserted. I was sent to track them down with half a dozen Apache Scouts. We found them . . . naturally. I was a fool to turn them over to him."

"Why?"

He opened his eyes. "One of them made a break for it when he saw Reno. Reno shot him down like a bird on the wing, using a long range rifle with telescopic sights. He thought it was a great joke."

She turned her head away. "And the others?"

"One of them hung himself rather than let Reno get his hands on him."

"And the third man?"

He wiped the sweat from his battered face.

"Most of the Apache Scouts were loyal. Several of them were bribed by Reno, with the use of whiskey and repeating rifles, to take the third man out into the desert, and to take care of him there.

"I found what was left of him, Lila. He had nothing but a spark of life left in him then, but he could talk."

"So?"

The hard gray eyes held hers. "It seems as though Reno had been interested in the man's wife and the man had found out."

She shook her head. "I knew he was anything but sterling," she said quietly, "but this is too much."

He got up on an elbow. "I turned him in. Of course the case was watered down. The United States Army couldn't let publicity like that get into the papers. He was asked to resign. It was the same as being cashiered. He never forgave me for it. Later I left the service to take up ranching."

She bathed his face. "Why are you here?" she asked.

"It doesn't concern you."

"Does it concern *them?*" She jerked her head toward the main part of the house.

60

"No."

"Are you lying to me?"

"No."

She wrung out the cloth in the basin. Then she looked at him. What if he was part Indian, as the others thought he was? Perhaps part Apache. He was as dark skinned as some of them she had seen, but the startling contrast of his gray eyes seemed to belie the charge.

She bandaged his lacerated scalp and stepped back. He took her by the hands. "You don't believe me, do you?" he asked quietly.

"I didn't say that."

"What do you think I am?"

"I don't know."

"But you don't trust me."

She took the basin and the cloths and walked to the door. She turned. "The only thing by which I can judge you is by what you did for Kathy. You risked your life to save her. It would have been easier to let them have her. You are something other than what they think you are. What it is I don't know, but I'm basing my belief in you on what you did for my sister."

The door closed behind her. Ken touched the bandage on his head. He wondered what Maynard Reno was telling the others. What was

Reno doing here? Ken knew one thing for sure. If they were up to anything below board he'd never live to get out to the desert.

He dropped on the bunk and closed his eyes. He needed rest. The time would come for a showdown quickly enough.

The moonlight made the night almost as bright as daylight. A coyote howled softly from the slopes of the butte and as his melancholy voice died away the cry was echoed from the west. Then the cry came from the south, near the canyon entrance.

Now Ken Driscoll stood at the window of his cell, with a cigarette pasted to the corner of his mouth. He nodded. The place was alive with Apaches. It was not their way to attack at night. The dawn raid, the stealthy evening ambush was their way of battle. But they held Bold Butte Ranch in a ring of warriors, and no one could get in or out of the canyon without them seeing or hearing him.

Reno had brought Amy Ives and her maid, Dorotea, with him, as well as four other men. The Apaches must have seen them out on the desert below Bold Butte, ripe for the picking, and yet Reno had come confidently into the canyon. With him he had brought four pack mules, heavily laden with goods of some kind or another. He was a trader, or so Slim had said. *Trading with whom?*

Then there was Jonce Ives, a rancher, or so *he* said, squatting on his ranch in the very mouth of the Bold Butte country where no white man had even been able to settle before. What was it he had said? *I ain't had no trouble with them since I been here. I never bother them—they never bother me.* But why? *Why?*

None of them at the ranch seemed particularly concerned about the Apaches, although they made a pretense of it. Reno gave the orders to Jonce Ives, or so Morgan Vestel had said. It was a cinch that Amy Ives had Jonce under her pretty thumb.

Whatever they were up to, it boded no good for Ken . . . Lila had said that. How had he gotten himself mixed up with such a hardcase *corrida?*

Ken heard the grating of feet on the roof over his head as the sentry paced back and forth. But as far as Ken could tell, there was only one man on duty as sentry. There was no one at the corral watching the animals, first target for raiding bucks. Horses for riding and mules for eating, and that meant a hell of a lot more to them than most things, with the exception of good trade knives and repeating rifles, with the other possible exception of white man's whiskey.

"Jesus!" said Ken suddenly.

Whiskey! The Bold Butte country had been the last place he would have suspected whiskey running. Yet Jonce Ives was there, at the very front door of the Apache stronghold, with good animals in his corrals, women and plenty of loot for marauding Apaches.

Jonce Ives or Maynard Reno was behind the whiskey running. They had to be. The pieces of the puzzle began to slip into place.

He rolled another cigarette and lighted it and as he raised his head he saw the kid walk toward the corrals. Niles Dunlap was his full name. Maybe Ken had a chance to get the kid to help him. On the other hand he had seen kids like Dunlap who were as deadly as men twice their age in that wild country.

Ken looked up at the butte. It couldn't be Nachee's band. They were raiding far south along the San Carlos the last Ken had heard. Diabolito was to the northwest, along the Verde. That left one band, that of Loco, and the thought formed a ball of ice in Ken's guts.

Loco had earned his name well. He was crazed enough as it was, and liquor made him a demon straight from hell. It was Loco's band which had raided Ken's place on Lost Creek.

The thought made him grip the bars and bow his head as the picture came again across his mind. Sweat broke out on his forehead as he tried to erase the picture, but it was no use.

"Ah God!" he husked.

"What's wrong, Driscoll?"

The voice broke through his thoughts and he opened his eyes to see the puzzled face of Niles Dunlap through the bars.

"What's wrong?" the kid asked again.

"Nothing, kid."

"Reno gave you a helluva going over."

"You're reminding me?"

"You won't ever forget."

"No."

The kid looked back over his shoulder. "I would have stopped him if I had been there."

"He'd have killed you."

The kid shook his head. "He's yellow, Driscoll."

Ken nodded. The kid had insight. Like all bullies and sadists, Maynard Reno was a coward at heart, but a deadly sort of coward at that.

"Niles!" The voice was that of Jonce Ives.

The kid turned. "You'd better get out of this place, Driscoll," he said over his shoulder.

"Sure. Sure," said Ken dryly.

The kid turned a little and spoke out of the side of his mouth. "I'll give you a hand if I can." Then he was gone.

"Where the hell you been?" demanded Jonce from the doorway of the house.

"Busy," said Niles.

"Well, you jump the next time I call you or I'll take a wheel spoke to you."

Ken rubbed his bristly jaws. The kid was with him, or had said he was, but there had to be a reason for it.

The coyote howled from the slopes of Bold Butte. The wind whispered down the canyon. Beyond that there was nothing but silence, but Ken had a feeling, and the feeling had never failed him yet. The heights and the dark parts of the canyon below the butte were thick with Apaches.

8

THE firelight flickered fitfully on the walls of the big living room, and now and then it lit the faces of the people in the room with bold relief. They were all there, with the exception of the women. Lila Ives was with her sister, in their room off the kitchen. Amy Ives was with her Mexican maid, Dorotea, in her room.

Maynard Reno stood with his back to the fireplace, warming his hands behind him. His protuberant blue eyes wandered from one man to the other.

Jonce Ives raised his glass and downed his whiskey. "We got nothing on Driscoll," he said at last.

Reno's tic worked a little. He looked at Morgan Vestel.

Vestel yawned. "Kill him," he said. "Don't take chances."

Federico was honing his slim *cuchillo*. He tested the edge of the blade with his thumb. "Why have his death on our souls?" he said softly. He jerked the knife toward the general direction of the butte. "Turn him loose without his horse and his weapons. *They* will take care of him."

"Not bad," said Slim. He wet his lips.

The kid leaned against the wall with his thumbs hooked over his wide gunbelt. They all looked at him. "I'll have nothing to do with it," he said quietly.

"Yellow?" jeered Morgan Vestel.

"Try me, you big bastard!"

The big man grinned.

Jonce looked at the four men who had come with Reno. Jack Vanbrugh was hardcase and had worked with Reno for a long time. He drew his left hand across his throat.

Reno raised his head and eyed the other three men. "Mawson?" he said.

Mawson was a little cluck-eyed man. He wet his lips. "I don't even know the man," he said.

"Maybe he can put a noose around your neck."

"All right then! Kill him and have done with it!"

"Lambert?" asked Reno.

Lambert emptied his glass. "You know me, Reno. Get rid of him. I knew him in the army.

He ain't here because he's running away. He came here looking for something. Maybe he don't know anything yet. I know one thing for sure: We let him live and we'll be signing our own death warrants."

The last was a dark, man with heavy features. 'Breed was written all over him. He looked around the room and the firelight seemed to glisten on his yellowish eyes.

"Tequila?" asked Reno.

Tequila drew a knife from his belt. He nodded.

Reno smiled thinly. He looked at the others. "There's your answer. Tequila would do it, but I won't let him."

"Why?" asked Jonce. "Let's get it over with!"

Reno shook his head. "I want something special for *Mister* Driscoll."

Jonce refilled his glass and then shoved the bottle toward Morg Vestel. "Damn it, Reno! One way or the other, but let's get the job over with!"

The kid walked toward the door.

"Wait!" said Vestel.

Niles turned slowly. "I don't want to be here when it's done," he said.

"Wouldn't put it past you to try and help him," said Vestel.

Reno turned his head a little and his glance struck the kid like a blow. "Just let him try," he said thickly.

A faggot snapped in the fireplace and a shower of sparks shot from it. Vestel poured a drink and downed it. They sat there eyeing each other.

Slim stood up. "I say we keep him here awhile. I don't want his death on *my* conscience."

"Crap on your conscience," said Morg Vestel.

Jonce nodded. "Yeh," he said. "Let's let it wait awhile, Reno. After all, he can't get away, and if he *did* get away he wouldn't get far."

Reno spat thickly. He walked to the door and opened it. For a moment he looked back into the room, then he slammed the big door closed behind himself.

Jonce stood up. "Let's get the stuff into the house," he said, "before Loco comes here looking for it. If he sees it sitting out there he might not bother to make a deal with us."

"I don't trust him," said Morg.

Slim grinned. "He sure as hell doesn't trust us," he said.

They all walked outside.

Niles Dunlap came into the big living room. He looked about, tiptoed to the door which led toward Amy Ives' room and then listened. Then quickly he went to a corner of the room, got Ken Driscoll's Colt and gunbelt, then left the room by the northern door.

Boots grated on the hard earth outside Ken's window. There was a scrabbling noise and as he turned he saw a hand reach between the bars with a holstered Colt. The Colt dropped with a thud on the floor. A moment later a sheathed bowie dropped atop it. Ken's feet hit the floor and he jumped to the window but there was no one there. A shadowy form vanished behind a pile of lumber.

Ken snatched up the weapons. It was his own belt and Colt, but the bowie was strange to him. He checked the Colt. It was fully loaded. He hid the belt in a corner beneath a pile of sacking, then placed the pistol under his thin mattress. The knife he hefted in his hand. It would take a long time to pick out the bars from the thick adobe, and besides the window

71

faced the courtyard and there was always someone walking around out there.

He paced back and forth. Once out in the open he had a fair chance of making Fort Ballard on foot, traveling by night and hiding by day, but he had no evidence as yet that the ranch was a base for the whiskey runners.

He glanced out of the window. They were in the big walled corral, working by lantern light. That itself was enough to show they did not fear the Apaches, unless they were outright damned fools.

Ken dropped onto his bunk and rolled himself a quirly with the last crumbs of his tobacco. He lighted the quirly and watched the smoke drift through the little window.

The low hum of voices came to him. He walked to the window and took his cigarette from his mouth, holding it cupped in his hand. Four men were crossing the courtyard carrying heavy burdens, but he could not make out what they were.

He stood there for twenty minutes watching the constant transferral of something from the corral to the house. The moon was on the wane and deep shadows filled the great canyon. The moon was gone when at last the work was finished. The lantern was doused in the corral and then two men came from there. Jonce Ives and Maynard Reno.

The two men stopped in front of the house. "Double their wages," said Jonce.

Reno spat. "Like hell!"

Jonce rubbed his jaws. "You think they might get riled up and talk when they get back?"

Reno shoved back his white hat. "They won't get back," he said quietly.

Jonce glanced swiftly at the house. "You mean?"

"You know damned well what I mean!" Reno shook a big fist. "I paid them good wages to help me get that stuff in here, and every rotten trip for the past three trips they upped their wages. Now this time they want a cut on the profits. I'll be damned if I'll do it!"

Jonce shook his head doubtfully. "They're all hardcase boys, Reno."

Reno laughed. "I don't figure on taking them on all at the same time. Tequila will do the work for me."

"And what about him?"

Reno smiled thinly. He opened and closed his big hands. "Dead men tell no tales," he said.

"I don't know, Reno. You left town with four men. You show up there without them and somebody is going to ask questions."

Reno spat again. "Jesus," he said patronizingly, "you don't use your head except to keep your ears apart! Now listen! The whole damned country is alive with Apaches. Nachee, Diabolito and Loco are raising hell all over. Now there are plenty of men getting ambushed by those three hellions. Don't you think it's possible that Lambert, Vanbrugh, Mawson and Tequila might be ambushed by our red brethren?"

Jonce looked puzzled.

Reno shook his head. "I often wonder how you ever made a *centavo* in this business until I came in with you, Jonce."

"Go to hell!"

The rancher opened the door and slammed it behind him.

9

ANOTHER day had passed. A long, hot day during which it had seemed as though the whole country was watching and waiting for something to happen, but nothing *had* happened.

Ken Driscoll stood at his window in the gathering twilight. None of the men were in sight. Now and then he heard the heavy footfalls of the sentry on the roof. During the day most of the men had come and gone, riding into the canyons on errands of which Ken had no inkling.

There had been no trace of smoke on the immense butte; no sign of the Apaches. Nothing but silence and heat.

Maynard Reno was out in the hills somewhere, with three of his men. Jonce Ives was on the lower slopes of the range to the west of the canyon cutting timber. He had not yet returned with his men. As far as Ken knew the only man about the place was Morgan Vestel, and he was doing sentry-go on the roof.

Out in the gathering twilight a coyote howled softly as he began his night's hunting.

The key turned suddenly in the lock and Ken whirled swiftly, dropping his right hand down to the top of his moccasin, where he had concealed the bowie knife, Apache fashion.

"*Quien es?*" The soft feminine voice surprised Ken. He stared into the dimness and saw a Mexican girl.

"Who are you?" asked Ken.

"Dorotea, maid to Mrs. Ives, *señor.*"

Ken snapped a match on his thumbnail and eyed her. He whistled softly, then lighted the candle stub on the rickety table.

She was well-shaped, slim and brown, with small but rounded breasts showing through the thin material of the white *camisita* she wore. A silver cross dangled in the cleft between her breasts. She placed a plate and a cup on the table and stood back, eyeing him half fearfully.

"Where is Miss Ives?" he asked.

"She would not bring it. Perhaps she is afraid of a lobo like yourself."

Ken grinned. "Are you not afraid too, *mi vida?*"

"No! Now eat."

Ken bowed and placed a chair beside her.

76

"Keep me company, Dorotea, I do not like to eat alone."

She stared at him for a moment and then sat down, crossing her slim legs. *"Gracias, señor,"* she said.

"It is nothing. You have eaten?"

"Yes."

He sat down and began to eat. He had had nothing all that day but some bread and water brought to him by the 'breed who had come with Maynard Reno. It had seemed to Ken that the man was sizing him up for the kill.

When he was done eating he felt in his pocket for the makings, then remembered he had used the last of them.

She thrust a slim hand inside her blouse. "Tobacco?" she asked.

He eyed her breasts appreciatively as she drew out her tobacco flask and handed it to him. It was still warm from her body. *"Gracias,"* he said with a smile. He took two of the brown papers from the flask and rolled two cigarettes, one of which he placed between her soft lips. He lighted both cigarettes, then sat back on his bunk, leaning against the wall.

"Where are the ladies?" he asked at last.

"Senorita Ives is with her sister, the poor

little one. Senora Ives is in her room resting. She is tired. The ride was long and her husband kept trying to get into her room last night. She would not let him." She laughed gayly. "He was like the mad bull last night."

"Who can blame him?"

She turned her head and spat. "From her he gets nothing. She is like the ice on the streams in the wintertime; ice on the top, and nothing but cold water beneath it."

"And you?"

She eyed him quickly, then threw her cigarette butt on the floor. "Make me another," she said.

"You did not answer me, *mi vida*."

"Time will tell."

"With me? I have little time."

"That is true."

"They mean to kill me, do they not?"

She studied him as he rolled a cigarette. "Does it matter? If you stay here they will kill you; if you leave the Apaches will kill you."

He smiled as he placed the cigarette between her lips. "Perhaps I too will do a little killing."

She paled a little.

"Do you want to see me die, little one?"

"No! *Santa Madre de Dios!* How can you say such a thing?"

"Then leave the door open when you go."

"They would kill me too then."

He looked down at his big dirty hands. "Perhaps I too can do a little killing," he said again. He grinned like a hunting wolf, slowly turning his head from side to side, and the resemblance was startling.

She jumped up quickly and the chair fell to the floor. Her eyes were wide in her pretty face.

Ken leaned back against the wall. "I can kill you easily and walk across your twitching body to that door and through it to safety."

She screamed shrilly.

Boots scraped on the roof and then came the creaking of the ladder as big Morg Vestel came down it to the ground.

"You see?" she said. She grinned too, as Ken had done, turning her head from side to side and accurately mimicking his imitation of a hunting wolf. Then she was at the door as Vestel called hoarsely down the hallway. Dorotea turned. "I am afraid here," she said in a low voice. "Those Apaches put the fear of God into my soul and bones. Perhaps I will be back."

He opened his mouth to speak but she quickly shut the door. A moment later he heard her curse in the hallway. He walked to the door and listened to the struggle going on out there and then he heard the ripping of cloth and heard Vestel spit out a filthy oath. The girl laughed and then Ken heard the other door, which led into the big living room, slam hard behind her. He heard Vestel follow her, cursing.

Ken listened to the sound of the heavy footfalls and then he heard another door open and close. It was getting darker and still none of the other men had returned to the ranch. Now Ken knew Ives had some sort of a deal with Loco, for the crazed chieftain would never have allowed white men to prowl about in the dusk without having them ambushed.

Ken looked up toward the butte. There was a naked rock shoulder which thrust itself out from the north end of the butte top and he could see the flickering of light upon it. Firelight—and he knew well enough the fires were not made by white men. Not up there at least.

He heard the soft thudding of hoofs up the canyon, and within a few minutes he knew all of the men, at least, he *thought* all of the white men, had returned.

"Evening mess," said Jonce Ives loudly from near the front door. "Lila has steaks and Mex strawberries."

"Anybody seen Mawson?" called out Jack Vanbrugh.

"He was with me near the spring an hour ago," said the man named Lambert.

It was dark in the courtyard except for the occasional glow of a cigarette lighting up a hard face.

Ken wet his lips. Maybe the Apaches had picked up one of them.

"Apaches?" asked Slim nervously.

Maynard Reno laughed. "Yeh," the ex-officer said, "that's it! Apaches."

Slim cleared his throat. "They never bothered us before," he said thickly.

"He'll probably be along later," said Jonce.

"Yeh," said Reno. Suddenly there was a spurt of yellow light as he snapped a match on his thumbnail and then held it to ignite the cigar in his mouth. The flare of light was just enough to show the impassive face of the 'breed who stood beside Reno, then the light was gone,

81

and Ken Driscoll knew well enough what had happened to the man named Mawson.

The big house was quiet except for the occasional creaking of a rafter as it complained of the coolness of the night. A soft wind pawed about the house and waved the brush on the slopes.

Ken Driscoll stood at his window. The confinement was getting to be too much for him. Then something struck his wandering mind. He turned suddenly and walked to the door. He remembered hearing Dorotea turn the key but he had not heard her withdraw it from the big lock. She'd been too busy fighting off Morg. He knelt on the filthy floor and picked up a straw. He poked it into the lock and it struck something rather than passing easily through.

Cold sweat broke out on his body. Yes! She had been so damned busy with Vestel she had left the key!

Ken wiped the sweat from his face. She'd be back sooner or later.

The key tantalized him. The door was too thick and made of too hard a wood for him to pick his way through with his knife.

He squatted on his heels and stared at the door, almost invisible in the darkness.

Ken suddenly reached down to the bottom of the door. It didn't quite reach the floor. There was a gap of about three-eights to half an inch between the bottom of the door and the floor.

He stood up and walked to his bunk. He dumped over the lumpy mattress and quickly cut a rectangle of the stout ticking material from the bottom covering. The piece of cloth was about as wide as the door and about three feet long. He took it to the door and patiently began to shove it underneath, using a slat he had found under the mattress. It took a long time to shove the stubborn material beneath the door, but at last he succeeded.

He sat back on his haunches, hesitating. He could not drive himself to the next thing he must do.

He whittled a stick from the slat and then knelt by the door, inserting the end of the stick in the lock until it touched the end of the key.

Ken closed his eyes and made a silent prayer with the sweat dripping from his face and running down his sides, then he shoved on the stick. The key held a little, then gave way and he heard it strike in the hallway.

He dropped the stick and bent to grip the edge of the ticking. Slowly he began to draw it back into the room.

Maybe the key had missed the material. Maybe it was too big to fit under the door. Maybe . . . maybe . . . maybe . . . Something struck the edge of the door and his heart seemed to skip a beat. He wanted to thrust his fingers beneath and touch that damned key but he knew he couldn't get them beneath the door. He reached for the stick and passed it slowly along beneath the door until he touched something. It was the key. It *had* to be the key!

He squatted for a minute, then began to draw in on the material once more. He didn't dare feel along the edge for a moment and then he did so and his fingers touched the cold metal of the key. He drew it in and gripped it so tightly he almost bent it.

Swiftly he eased the key into the lock, turned it softly, then stepped out into the hallway. Something warned him. He kicked the material back into the room, closed the door and locked it, then stood close to the door inside the room, listening and waiting.

It didn't take long. He heard the other door ease open, then the soft husking noise of sandals, then the quick breathing just outside the door and the touch of something against the lock.

"*Canalla!*" she said, and then she was gone. Ken grinned. She was sure now she had removed the key, but she thought she had lost it or misplaced it. *Bueno!* Let her sweat it out when Jonce Ives or Maynard Reno asked for the key. Maybe they had a duplicate. Ken hoped so. It would make it easier on what he planned to do.

He quickly formed a shape on the mattress, composed of anything he could find in the room, until it looked like a human figure lying there. He stretched the thin blanket over it. He buckled on his gunbelt, checked the Colt once again, then left the room, locking it behind him. The knife he kept in his hand. It might be needed and was a lot quieter by far than the butt of a Colt or the crashing discharge of a cartridge.

He walked toward the big living room and stood there for a moment with his hand on the handle, listening like a great, lean lobo, then he turned the handle and eased the door back.

The big living room was dark except for a fitful winking ember in the thick bed of ashes in the fireplace. The mingled odors of whiskey, spicy food, woodsmoke and stale sweat hung in the room. A man snored softly from the far side of the fireplace.

Ken stood there, testing the darkness with his senses, and the thick-bladed bowie was held in his right hand, blade uppermost for a sure hard thrust.

The impulse was strong in him to get out of there . . . now!

He fought to control the desire to escape. Surely one, or more of them, was on guard outside. In Apache country, during troubled times, most ranches, stage stations and isolated places kept fifty percent of their men on guard. But not at Bold Butte Ranch.

He padded out into the room, feeling his way along, hoping he wouldn't tread on someone lying on the floor, because now he knew there were a number of sleepers in the room.

It would be loco to poke about in the room with men like those sleeping there. They were frontiersmen, alert as cats, and he had been damned lucky as it was to get as far as he had.

The part of the house Ken had been in, the eastern arm of the U, consisted of small rooms, probably intended for travelers on the stage line. Therefore, it was reasonable to assume that the owner's quarters, and the supply room or rooms, were either just west of the big living room, or in the western arm of the U.

He padded to the door and stopped to listen. He wondered if Jonce Ives was with his luscious wife. She was quite a filly!

He tested the door handle. It let down easily and the heavy door swung open. A cool draft played on his sweaty face. He stepped into the darkness beyond the door. The walls were thick and soundproof. The station had been built well, a veritable fortress in miniature; a citadel beneath Bold Butte.

A faint touch of light showed down the hallway. The moon was probably rising.

He rested his head against the first door to his left and in a little time he heard soft breathing. He padded on to the next room but heard nothing.

The doors on the right-hand side of the hallway were all locked. He kept on until he reached the west wall and then looked down the hallway to his left, trying to pierce the thick darkness, lighted only a little bit by moonlight coming in through a loophole at the southern end of the hallway.

The hallway was littered with trash. Three of the four small rooms were unlocked and their windows shuttered. The light of a match revealed more trash, sacks of grain, furniture, saddles and other horse furnishings.

The fourth room opened to him easily when he pried at the lock with the heavy blade of his bowie. The reek of kerosene came to him as he lighted a match and he half expected a spurt of flame from the thick fumes. The room was piled with kerosene cans. He scratched his jaw. Jonce Ives sure used a lot of the stuff.

Ken went back into the hallway and up it to the first door which opened on the east-west hallway. The door was locked. He tried it with the key he had taken from the door of his own room. The lock moved a little. He put pressure on the key and with a slight grating noise the door opened to him.

He closed the door behind him and lighted a match. There were no windows in the large room and the loopholes were sealed with thick wooden covers. The room was well filled with supplies. Sacks and barrels; kegs and crates; bundles and stacks. Jonce seemed to have a considerable amount of money tied up in supplies, but then he was a long way from the nearest supply source, and probably bought in quantity. But it took money . . . *lots* of money, and again the thought struck Ken, there was no obvious means of income at the isolated ranch.

He lighted more matches and poked about. Dust was thick on everything. Most of the supplies had been there for some time, although it didn't take long for dust to accumulate in that country.

If there was whiskey stored in the ranch house it was either somewhere in the living room, or in one of the women's rooms, and the last wasn't likely.

Ken left the room and locked the door behind him.

He padded down the hallway and then froze as he heard a door open. He could dimly make out a figure walking down the hallway away from him. It stopped at the end door, and knuckles rapped gently on the wood.

Ken stepped back into a doorway and pressed back against the door.

The knuckles rapped again. "Amy?" It was the hoarse voice of Jonce Ives.

The poor bastard, thought Ken. He grinned.

The light seemed a little brighter in the hallway now. The moon was rising fast.

Ken could hear Jonce's hard breathing and then a soft, muttered curse.

Then there was the soft sound of footsteps and a clicking noise. Jonce had given up—for that night at least.

Ken wiped the sweat from his face. His night foray had done him little good. His next move was uncertain. He could go back to his room and lock himself in, then take Jonce or Reno as hostages if they came to him, but the odds were too high that way, and there were too many hardcases staying at the ranch.

He could slip out of the house and get into the hills, then wait his chance to find out what was going on at Bold Butte Ranch, but then there was the hazard of Loco and his keen warriors to contend with.

He padded down the hallway and eased open the door to the living room. It was lighter in there now, with shafts of pale moonlight protruding through the loopholes, and in the light he could see blanketed forms on the floor. There were five men sleeping there, which left three unaccounted for, Jonce being in his room.

Ken turned into the kitchen. He helped himself to dried meat and fruit, matches and tobacco from the stores in the pantry. A canteen hung from a hook near the door which opened onto the patio. He took it and left the kitchen, standing close to the east wall of the patio, listening for the footfalls of a guard.

There was no sound except the sighing of the wind about the house. The moonlight was brighter, and in a little while it would fill the patio area with silvery light.

Ken walked softly toward the wide gateway which opened onto the canyon. He reached it, then heard the noise of a footfall on the roof just above him. "That you, Tequila?" It was the voice of Frank Lambert, a man Ken had known at Fort Ballard. A deserter and thief.

"Tequila?" The voice came again.

Ken turned a little and looked up. He could just see the broad shoulders and the large hat outlined against the moonlight, but Ken was in darkness. "Yes," he said softly.

"What you doing?"

"Listening, just listening."

Lambert leaned farther over the edge of the low parapet. "You're acting damned suspicious," he said.

"Listen," said Ken.

Lambert turned his head a little and at that moment Ken leaped up, hooked a hand over the parapet, swung up a leg and then gripped Lambert by the scarf about his neck. Ken pulled hard, released his hold on the parapet and dropped to the ground, twisting the scarf as he did so. There was a muffled gasp from the half-strangled man.

Lambert was big and strong, a veteran of barroom brawls and behind-the-stables encounters for a good many years. He released his hold on his rifle and butted Ken with his head, driving him back against the wall with a thud. There was no time to waste fighting with the man. He could arouse the whole place in a matter of seconds.

Lambert opened his mouth as he swung at Ken with both fists. Ken freed his bowie, stepped in under the flailing arms and drove the knife upward just beneath the left side of the rib cage. "Ah!" choked Lambert. He fell forward and lay still.

Ken tried to curb his harsh breathing. It had been a close thing. But not a sound came from the house.

Ken gripped the man by his scarf and dragged him to a ladder. He hoisted him to his back and made his slow way up the creaking wooden structure, hoping to God it didn't collapse beneath the heavy weight.

He dumped Lambert on the roof and looked closely at his face. The eyes were already glazing.

Ken crawled to the parapet just above the courtyard. There wasn't a sign of life down there. A horse whinnied softly from the walled corral.

Ken crawled back and searched through Lambert's clothing, taking his field glasses, tobacco, matches and a double handful of rifle cartridges from it. Ken went down the ladder, picked up Lambert's Winchester, then softly opened the wide gateway. Maybe they'd think Apaches had killed Lambert. In time they'd learn that Ken was no longer a prisoner and then they'd know who had killed the ex-soldier. The man was no loss, but Ken would have had it otherwise, rather than to have killed him.

He faded into the brush, climbing up the western slopes just west of the house, keeping to the shelter of brush and trees, steadily working his way a little northerly until he was high on a ledge over the canyon just as the moon began to fill it with clear silvery light.

From where he was he could see everything.

The springs up the branch canyon; the ranch buildings; Bold Butte and its approaches; the wide mouth of the canyon and the silvered desert beyond. He could see too, the huddled shape of the dead man on the roof of the house.

10

THE sun was warm on his back when he woke up. He rolled over and looked down into the canyon. Smoke drifted up from the big chimney of the house. A man stood on the roof, leaning on a rifle. He was looking up toward Bold Butte.

Ken wet his mouth from the canteen, then slowly ate the meat and fruit he had taken from the kitchen. While he ate he kept his eyes on the house. Now and then a man passed through the courtyard, and once he saw a woman walk through the patio.

He wet his mouth again and then uncased the field glasses he had taken from Lambert's body. He focused them and studied the house. They were good glasses, of German make, and they showed the rooftop almost as though he was within fifty yards of it. There was a dark stain on the roof where he had left the body of Frank Lambert.

He studied the canyon foot by foot, shading the glasses with his hat so that the morning sun wouldn't reflect from the lens. It was peaceful down there. Some of the horses had been taken from the corral and were picketed on the western slopes of the butte for grazing. Now Ken knew damned well that Jonce Ives had some sort of deal with the Apaches.

He lay there a long time. Jonce Ives and Maynard Reno were obviously in a partnership in the whiskey-running, if it *was* whiskey-running they were doing. Jonce kept the place as a front while Reno brought in the goods; *wet* goods. Amy Ives must cost Jonce a pretty sum in *dinero* for him to take such risks. Any man who had such a place as Bold Butte Ranch, provided the Apaches were peaceful, had a potential gold mine. Ken had seen few such places with the advantages it had.

He cast his eyes up at the butte. A shimmering haze already hung about it, giving it an unreal quality, as though it was being seen in a dream.

He trained his glasses on the springs, and drew in his breath sharply. There were men standing on the rock-shelf over the mouth of the flow of water. There was no mistaking them. Their thick manes of hair gave their heads an enormous look and their squat, powerful bodies made them look like trolls who had suddenly appeared from the bowels of the butte. Apaches, a dozen of them at least. High above the party, at intervals along the steep winding trail, could be seen other warriors, watching the springs far below.

Ken shaded the glasses as he studied face after face. He was sure they couldn't see him, but it never payed to take chances with them.

He turned to look at the house again. Men were in the courtyard, loading burros and horses with something. He adjusted the glasses and saw Maynard Reno, Jonce Ives, Jack Vanbrugh and the 'breed, Tequila, standing there. In a short time they led the animals through the gateway and toward the springs.

Ken wiped the sweat mist from the glasses and looked again at the springs. Some of the Apaches had come down from the rock-shelf and were squatting near the first water pan of the spring, with their rifles across their thighs.

The Apaches made no move toward the white men as they neared the lower water pan.

The white men began to unload the animals, piling dark colored cans beside the waters. Ken studied the cans. They looked familiar, and then the thought struck him. They looked exactly like the kerosene cans he had seen in the small room at the house, but they had smelled of the fuel, not of whiskey.

Some of the Apaches had come forward and were talking to the 'breed, who in turn spoke to Reno. It took a long time. The sun was flooding the canyon now and the heat of it rose to where Ken was hidden.

Some of the Apaches had come to the pile of cans and each of them took one, hoisted it to his shoulder, then started up the long steep trail toward the top of the butte. But there were several of the Apaches still talking through Tequila and making motions with their hands.

Reno pointed toward the desert, up the canyon, and then almost directly toward the place where Ken was hidden. One of the Apaches nodded. He turned and spoke to two of his mates. The white men started back toward the ranch house.

In a little time Apaches began to drift away from the springs, and then they were gone. By the time the white men had reached the house and disappeared from sight, there was no human to be seen except the motionless guard on the roof of the house.

An unnatural silence hung over the canyon.

Ken cased his glasses. There was no need for him to wonder where the Apaches had gone. They were hunting. Slipping through the brush and rocks like *chisos*; phantoms on a hunt for something, and that something was Ken Driscoll.

The next day Ken Driscoll had kept high on the canyon side, shifting his position only when he knew the human bloodhounds searching for him were getting too close for comfort. Now, with the coming of dusk, he had holed up for a breather in a cave whose entrance was thickly screened with brush and scrub trees.

Even in his hideout he could hear the faint throbbing of the drums. The pattern was repeating itself. The raiders slashed their way across the country for a week or ten days, then would vanish for about two weeks, only to reappear and start the process all over again. Loco's boys were building up their store of hate and greed atop the butte, and when the right moment came, they would lance down and reopen the gates of hell once more.

Ken stripped to trousers and moccasins, rebuckled on his gunbelt, passing the loop over the hammer spur and snapping it down. He might have to belly about a bit, and might have to run, and he couldn't afford to loose his six-shooter. His knife he carried in the top of his right moccasin. He bound a bandana about his thick hair and then rubbed wet earth over his face and upper body.

He squatted in the cave while the earth dried on his body. There was nothing else to do. He had no food left and only a little water, and he damned well better not smoke.

There was only one way to make sure what was in those black cans the Apaches had taken to the butte top, and that was to get up to the butte top itself if necessary.

Loco was too shrewd to let all of his bucks drink at the same time . . . there would be guards, as sober as deacons, along the butte trail.

Ken digested all of his thoughts. He'd be able to outwit a drunken Apache; he had done it before, for liquor took hold of them quite easily. But if he *was* caught . . . Ken closed his eyes and drove the thought from his mind. The deal was tough enough without him adding mental torture to make it worse.

The canyon was as black as the pit. High on

the butte the flickering firelight reflected from granite surfaces, and if one watched closely enough, he would see a faint, staggering shadow flit across the illuminated rock-faces.

Ken Driscoll raised his head, making sure there was thick darkness behind it, so that he wouldn't be silhouetted. The springs were far below him now, but he had not yet cleared the great talus slope, stippled with brush, trees and rock ledges, which lay like a great harsh blanket on the lower slopes of the northeast face.

It was the only way up. Everyone who knew that country knew there was only one way up. The northeast face had the only trail, and after it cleared the growths around the springs, it meandered across the talus slope. In the daytime a mouse couldn't work his way across that slope without being seen. At night sound carried far, and with the coming of moonlight, the slopes would be as bright as full daylight.

There were some hours before moonlight, but Ken Driscoll knew that he might make his way across the slopes by that time, but he'd be trapped there until the moon was gone, and he had no idea of what type of terrain it was. From a distance it looked like naked rock, probably creviced quite a bit, but still no place to be squatting with Apaches poking about.

Now and then he'd heard faint cries from the butte top and the steady throbbing of the drums never stopped. They were holding a witches' sabbath up there this night.

He tested the night with ears and eyes but it seemed as though he was all alone on the talus slope.

Ken bellied along a shallow hollow close to a tranverse ledge which thrust itself up above the talus. Then suddenly he stopped, sniffing the cool night air. The pungent odor of kerosene had drifted to him.

He inched along until the odor of the fuel became stronger and then he found the can lying to one side of the twisting trail. The can was empty. Ken felt sinking disappointment.

Ken looked up toward the butte top. The cans in the storeroom at the ranch, this can he had just found, and those Ives and Reno had taken to the Apaches down at the springs were identical. No ranch could possibly use so much kerosene in the time Ives had lived there.

It was a cinch one couldn't mix kerosene with liquor. Even an Apache wouldn't drink a mess like that. Apaches had no use for kerosene in their simple camp life. The only use they ever had for it was to splash it around when they took a ranch or a stage station, then touch it off for the roaring holocausts they loved to leave behind them as their trademark. But somehow the whiskey and kerosene had to have a connection.

This was his first and only lead. He turned his head and looked down toward the unseen springs. Jonce Ives and Maynard Reno had brought the kerosene cans to the springs and had given them to the Apaches. Reno had brought the latest stock of cans to the ranch. The ranch storeroom was full of such empty cans, all stinking of kerosene, not liquor.

Ken rubbed his bristly jaw. It was a cinch the two whiskey-runners hadn't given *all* of the last supply of whiskey to the Apaches. Therefore it must be that some of it was still at the ranch.

Now there was only one way to get his final proof; proof which would stand up in court.

He closed his eyes. He had two choices: go to the butte top and see if he could find out how the liquor got into Apache hands, which wouldn't be proof of a damned thing and would end with him losing his life. Or the second choice was to go back to the ranch and get conclusive evidence.

He was damned if he did and damned if he didn't.

There was a furtive movement up the trail. Ken pressed his body flat to the ground and felt for his knife.

Something moved behind him. He slowly turned his head and saw a dim figure twenty feet away from him, on the unseen trail.

Ken began to inch his way up the slope away from the trail. He reached out his left hand toward a rock to pull himself upward and his hand met warm metal. A second later the empty kerosene can fell into a cleft, rattled along the bottom, then fell noisily onto the rocky trail.

There was no sound of voices from the dim figures. They were Apaches, not white men, and not given to startled cries. Instead they closed in toward Ken.

Ken leaped to his feet, hurdled a rock ledge and started down a stony slope, sliding and stumbling in the loose talus rock. The noise was a clattering alarm signal to the Tontos. He heard their slurring speech, much closer than he thought it would be.

Unleashed power seemed to flow into his

muscular legs. He went down the slope like a steeplechase horse, clearing rocks and dimly seen crevices in his stride.

But they could run, too. They spent a good part of their lives climbing steep heights at high elevations which gave them tremendous powerful leg muscles and deep chests, well suited for the harsh country they lived in.

Ken angled back up the slope, found a flat stretch of unlittered rock and opened out almost to the limit of his speed. He was working away from the trail and keeping away from the springs. He was heading toward the southwest, out from the northwest corner of Bold Butte.

A soft cry came from behind and below him, to be followed by a similar cry from behind and above him. *There are still only two of them*, he thought. A moment later his hopes were dashed. Three more cries came to him on the vagrant breeze. Five of them, in the deadly pursuit.

He was below the bold western face of the great butte, with the cold moonlight flooding the canyon beneath him. There was no place to hide now, other than in the shadows of a crevice, for nothing could cross those lighted areas without being seen by the keenest eyes in the world.

Ken Driscoll lay at full length beside a ledge, trying to calm his harsh breathing. The blood hammered inside his aching skull. His legs were shaking a little from the exertion he had made in the past hours while he played hare and hounds with the Tontos on the rugged sides of Bold Butte.

He bent to the side and began to knead his legs.

He looked up at the western face of the butte. Deep gullies split the lower slopes, like shadowed areas on a summer's day, but close up they turned into devil's pockets, filled with crumbling rock and every kind of stinging, clinging, stabbing type of thorny vegetation known to that harsh country. There was a trace of a long, transverse ridge which slanted up the naked side of the butte like a pathway to the moon. It was impossible to tell exactly where it ended and whether or not it led up the top of the butte where Loco's bucks were having their hell's carnival that night.

The immense bulk of the butte almost made him dizzy as he stared up at it and he tore his mind away from it, for the cold realization had come to him that the moon would soon wane, allowing him a few hours of darkness before the coming of the dawn. When the dawn came he wouldn't stand a chance of eluding the searching Tontos. When the dawn came . . .

He worked his way down the deep crevice, feeling his way with torn and bleeding hands, hoping to God all the while that his questing fingers wouldn't touch the cold scaly body of a rattler that would strike faster than the speed of light to let him die horribly and alone on the merciless stone side of Bold Butte.

Now he was at the end of the crevice and before him was a rock-littered area between him and the thick brush and trees which bordered the east side of the canyon floor. He knew well enough that he could get across that area if only white men were looking about for him, but he could not drive himself across it now, knowing that the Apaches were somewhere behind him, perhaps even in the far end of the deep crevice itself.

He touched his cracked lips with his dry tongue. The ranch buildings were to his right up the silent canyon. It was the only place for him to go. The butte was unsafe; the desert would be a sunlit trap for him when the day came.

Ken closed his eyes and his big hands clenched and unclenched themselves in the coarse gravel.

His head snapped up as he heard the high-pitched voice cry out. "For God's sake! No!"

Ken turned his head. The voice had come from the slopes to his right.

It was silent again for a short time and then a hoarse bleating cry rose on the night air and echoed from the canyon walls. A horrid, animal-like sound, as though a sheep was being tortured.

The cold sweat broke out on Ken's naked upper body and trickled down his filthy sides.

"For Heaven's sake, Tequila! Tell them who I am!" the voice shrieked out. It rose high on a note at the end as though a honed knife had sliced into shrinking flesh.

The voice was familiar, thought Ken. He wiped the cold sweat from his face. They were so damned close. If they came fifty yards to the south they would stumble over him.

The voice shrieked again and then Ken recognized it. It was the voice of the man they called Van . . . Jack Vanbrugh. The man who had come first to the ranch that night, just ahead of Reno and the others.

Tequila was there too, for Vanbrugh had called out to him. Tequila, the cold-faced, yellow-eyed 'breed, who was like Maynard Reno's shadow. Tequila who had murdered the little, cluck-eyed man named Mawson.

Vanbrugh was sobbing and moaning now and the sounds were hardly human. The eerie part of the whole business was that not another voice was heard. The Apaches were working silently, but enjoying the sport none the less for that. Ken could picture them squatting about the writhing, naked body while each of them added his little knife cut in such a way that pain would be exquisite but that death would be held off a little longer.

Reno had told Jonce Ives that none of Reno's men would get back from the canyon. *I don't figure on taking them on all at the same time*, he had said. *Tequila will do the work for me.* Then Reno would take care of Tequila. Clever.

Mawson had been murdered. Ken had killed Lambert. Now Jack Vanbrugh was dying to make sport for blood-hungry bucks while Tequila waited to carry the news to Reno; and for his good news he would earn a slug of lead or the sharp tip of a knife.

Now Vanbrugh was moaning, and soon that too died away, and there was no sound but the soft night wind moaning through the trees and scrub brush.

There was nothing to see; neither sight nor sound of the Apaches. But they were still there, or perhaps were closing in on Ken at last.

He eased his hand down to his Colt and his questing fingers touched leather, but not steel and wood. He felt about on the harsh ground. The six-shooter was gone.

He looked back up the crevice. There was no chance in going back to look for it.

He drew out his knife. Perhaps they would miss him. Perhaps he could sprint for the canyon, but his legs were tired, and he knew they would outlast him.

The moon hung low in the west and already shadows were creeping across the slopes. But it was yet too early for the safe cover of darkness.

Ken bellied forward, away from the protecting crevice and the ring of rocks which held their grisly secret.

He was almost to the shelter of the trees when something made him turn his head. His blood ran cold and seemed to congeal in his skull. There were six of them in the dying moonlight. Six of them watching him, and they held their bloody knives in their hands.

He stood up with his blade ready for combat but he knew he didn't have a chance. Better to slash his own throat or hurl himself onto their blades than to be bound and taken to the top of that hellish butte.

Minutes ticked past as they stood there like figures carved on a stone frieze. They wanted him alive.

Something moved high on the slope. Ken looked up. It was another Apache. He came steadily down the slope, with a repeating rifle held in the crook of his left arm, and the moon shone on his broad face. It was the Apache who had been known to his own people as Toga-de-chuz, the madman who led his ferocious warriors through sheer terrorism and the domination of his insane will, thus earning for himself the name of Loco.

He knew Ken Driscoll. Loco had led the raid at Lost Creek. It was Loco's knife which had scarred Ken for life.

Loco spoke softly. His warriors nodded, but they did not take their eyes from the white man.

They spread out and approached him slowly, and two of them took slings from their moccasin-tops and stooped to pick up rounded stones the size of an egg.

Ken wet his lips. He knew those deadly slings. Apaches learned the use of them as boys. They could bounce a stone off his skull and knock him out for easy taking. He hadn't figured on this.

They were twenty yards from him now. Loco did not move.

Ken backed away, a foot at a time, watching for a chance.

They were fifteen yards away now and the two slingers placed their stones into the diamond-shaped pieces of rawhide and adjusted the two strings.

Ten yards, and the warriors stopped. The slingers drew back their arms.

The crashing report of the gun seemed inches from Ken's left ear, and his head rang with the noise. The foremost slinger went down, jerking and quivering.

The gun roared again and the second slinger staggered back gripping his right arm, while his sling hung loosely from his right hand.

Smoke drifted between Ken and the warriors.

He leaped to one side as Loco raised his rifle. *"Ahagahe!"* he yelled insanely.

Once more the gun spat flame and smoke and Loco leaped high in the air as a shard of stone slashed upward from where the bullet had struck and struck him on the left cheekbone, filling his eyes with tears.

Ken crashed through the shrubbery. The rifleman stood behind a slanted, sharp-edged boulder, firing steadily at the rest of the braves.

The Apaches were retreating, leaving three of their mates on the ground.

Ken ran toward his rescuer. He stared. It was a woman. She turned and he saw the pale oval face of Lila Ives. Ken took the hot rifle from her hands and raised it. He drove a shot after a running warrior and the heavy slug helped him on a pace or two until he fell dead.

Then the Apaches were gone, with their dead on the slopes behind them.

"Knife and awl!" yelled Ken in Apache. *"Knife and awl,* Toga-de-chuz!"

She swayed against him and he supported her with his free arm, helping her down the slope and into the thick grove of trees.

He gripped her by her upper arms and drew her close. "I don't know how or why you're here," he whispered "but you saved my life back there, Lila."

She looked up at him. "What else was I to do?" she said. "I was frightened. Frightened more than I have ever been in my whole life when I saw them standing there, staring at you with those terrible eyes, and when they closed in . . . I had to shoot."

He grinned crookedly. "And damned good shooting too," he said.

"Did you see her?" she asked tensely.

He looked down at her in surprise.

"Did you see her?" she demanded again.

"Who?"

"Kathy!"

"Where is she?" he asked thickly.

"She left the house to look for Patsy and I followed her. She came this way."

He turned and looked up the distant slopes, now vague and unreal in the dying moonlight.

A coyote howled softly.

She gripped him by the arms. "Did you see her?" she demanded fiercely, and her nails dug into his hard flesh.

The coyote howled again, and it seemed to be echoed by the faint cry of a female child. "Patsy! Patsy! Patsy!"

It was quiet for a time and then the girl called again. "Patsy!"

Lila turned to go but Ken held her back. She struggled fiercely but his hands held her like rawhide and steel and when she saw the look on his face she quieted down.

From somewhere, high on the rocky western slopes of Bold Butte a curious sound broke out, a demoniacal laughter. It died away.

"Who was that, Ken?" she asked huskily.

"Loco," he said. His eyes were wide in his head as he looked up the slopes.

The laughter came again, louder this time. "Knife and awl! Knife and awl!" called out Loco. His voice was followed by that of Kathy Ives as she screamed in sudden pain.

Loco was still laughing when Lila Ives slumped helplessly at Ken's feet.

11

THE moon was gone and the canyon below Bold Butte was dark and cold. The man and the woman stood in the shelter of a motte of timber and looked toward the ranch which was hardly distinguishable to them. Only the faint odor of woodsmoke let them know there was life in the great house.

"What will you do now?" she asked him.

Ken leaned against a tree. He had not told her why he had come to the Bold Butte country. He didn't believe she had anything to do with the whiskey-running, but it seemed hard to believe that such an intelligent and alert young woman could live at the ranch and *not* know what was going on there.

Lila Ives looked up into his dark face. "Why did you come here, Ken?"

He shrugged.

"You came here for a purpose, Ken. You're no drifter—no saddle tramp living from job to job and meal to meal."

"Why not?" he asked dryly.

"I know better."

She gripped his left arm. "Tell me!"

"There is nothing to tell."

"You're lying."

He looked toward the ranch. "Go home," he said.

"To what?" she asked bitterly.

"You must let them know Loco has Kathy."

She looked toward the ranch. "I think they must know by now. When I left I heard Maynard Reno tell Jack Vanbrugh and Tequila to follow me."

Ken rubbed his dirty jaws. "That figures."

"Why would Reno do such a thing? He cares nothing for Kathy."

He jerked a thumb back toward the way they had come. "It was a way for Reno to get rid of Vanbrugh."

"What do you mean?"

"Tequila killed Mawson at Reno's orders."

"You're lying again!"

"No," he said quietly. "Reno doesn't want any of his men to get out of here." He looked up toward the butte. "Mawson is dead. Vanbrugh is dead. Lambert is dead. Tequila hasn't long to live now that he's done his job."

"Who killed Frank Lambert?"

117

Ken wet his lips and looked away.

"*You* did, Ken."

"Yes," he said quietly.

"You're no better than Loco then! No better than Tequila!"

He drew her close and the pressure hurt her but she did not cry out. "Listen," he said fiercely. "You want to know why I came here? I'll tell you! Because the Bold Butte country was the one place no man had been able to penetrate in a hunt which has been going on for months. A hunt for the white slime who have been peddling rotgut to the Apaches.

"Nachee is bad and Diabolito is worse, but the worst of them is Loco, and with liquor he becomes a devil incarnate."

Her face was white as she listened. The wind shifted a little and began to blow a little harder, and it seemed to her as though she heard voices in the wind.

"Listen," he said again, and this time his voice was lower. "Your uncle's ranch is the headquarters for whiskey-running in this country."

"You lie!"

He held his face closer to her. "Reno brings in that whiskey and caches it here. Your uncle

118

lets Loco know when it is here and Loco comes here to his stronghold to get the whiskey."

She turned her face away from his.

He went on. "Why do you think the Apaches let your uncle stay here in this canyon? Why have they left his horses and mules alone? It's obvious, isn't it?"

She nodded. "Jonce was a good man. He was all right until he married Amy. He gave her great promises in Tucson. He spent every cent he had on her there and treated her royally and she came to believe he had money. Then he was broke but he couldn't resist asking her to marry him.

"He came to me. I had enough money from my father to pay for this ranch. It would be a home for Kathy and myself, and Jonce would leave it to us. It wasn't for myself that I was worried, but for Kathy. I knew nothing of this country. I knew there were Apaches here but Jonce didn't seem concerned. I wondered why he got such a ranch with the money he had, but I was happy for Kathy.

"It was Amy who worked on him, bleeding him for more and more money until the poor man nearly broke down."

Ken grunted deep in his throat.

"Yes," she said softly, "he's weak, but he wasn't a bad man, Ken."

He raised his right arm and pointed up toward the butte top. "They're sleeping off the father and mother of all drunks up there now," he said harshly. "What happens when they wake up with the father and mother of all hangovers?"

"Kathy," she said brokenly.

"There's a chance for her," he said. "If she acts as she has since I killed Patsy, they won't bother her. *Mind-gone-far*, is their term for it. They won't harm her, but they won't let her go, either."

"What can we do?"

"Maybe Loco will listen to Jonce or Reno. They have a hold on him, perhaps as much of a hold as anyone could have on that limb of Satan. They could hold off on his liquor supply until he gave her up."

"You think so?"

He looked down at her. "You might as well know the truth. Loco can take Bold Butte Ranch with a quarter of his strength in warriors."

"But he hasn't done so because of the fact he gets his liquor here?"

120

"If he attacks he knows no more liquor will be brought in."

"Then he should return Kathy."

The wind was cold on Ken Driscoll as he spoke. "He wants something for that little girl. He wants to bargain."

"What can he want?"

"*Quien sabe?* Who knows?"

Ken pointed to the ranch. "Go home now. Talk to Jonce. Have them send a messenger to Loco to see what he wants."

"And what about you?"

He smiled. "The son of man has no home, but I'll be close enough."

She hesitated. He bent and kissed her gently. "I'll get her back for you, Lila. I did it once before. I can do it again."

Her arms went around his neck, and she drew him close to kiss him with surprising strength and passion, and then she was gone into the darkness.

Ken Driscoll lay in the pungent-smelling brush, with his chin resting on his clasped hands, watching the ranch far below him. The canyon was peaceful under the late morning sun. The thought came to him again that the place would be a wonderful holding for a strong man in the years to come.

He had seen the 'breed, Tequila, leave the ranch at dawn and walk toward the springs, then up the trail toward the top of the butte. That had been hours ago. Now and then some of the people at the ranch had come from the house and had looked up at the butte, only to return into the house.

There was a movement on the butte trail and a solitary figure appeared, walking down toward the springs. Ken raised his glasses and focused them on the figure. The dark face of Tequila swam hazily into view. The man staggered a little now and then and as he reached the springs he drew out a canteen from beneath his filthy coat and raised it to his lips. He raised it higher and higher, then took it from his lips and hurled it into the brush. He stood there for a moment, then wiped his lips and lurched down toward the canyon floor.

Ken lowered the glasses. Tequila was on a high lonesome. What message did he bring from Loco?

Ken cased the glasses and slung them from his shoulder. He picked up one of his two repeating rifles and started down the side of the canyon toward the house. He hadn't seen a sign of an Apache all morning long. Loco was up to some sly game, and the thought of what he might have in mind sent a chill through Ken.

He squatted in the brush a hundred yards from the west side of the house. The place seemed peaceful enough. A mule bawled from the corral. Smoke drifted lazily from the great chimney.

Half an hour had passed when he saw Lila Ives appear alone on the flat roof. She looked toward the west, seemingly right over Ken's head, and he knew she wanted to speak with him.

Ken stood up in the brush, long enough for her to see him and then he sank down again.

She was there in minutes. Her face was pale and her hands trembled a little. He kissed her, "Well?" he asked.

"You were right," she said quietly. "He does want something for Kathy."

"What?"

She looked away.

"Lila!"

She bit her lip. He turned her face toward him. "What does he want?"

"You," she said quietly.

The warm wind seemed chilly now. "I thought so," he said.

She looked at him in surprise. "You knew all the time?"

"Yes."

"You could have run away."

He nodded.

"Those in the house know you are around here. They sent me to talk with you."

He grinned wryly. "Why didn't they all come?"

"I said I would talk with you first."

"For what end? To give myself up to that hellion on the butte? Do you know what he'll do to me?"

Her face was taut with emotion. "Why does he want you?"

"You saw him watching me last night. I killed some of his warriors at Lost Creek."

"Defending your home."

He shrugged. "That makes no difference to an Apache." He looked up at the sunlit butte. "Last night made my debt still greater to him, in his twisted way of reasoning. Kathy fell into his hands. He won't hurt her, but he knows you people won't believe that. As long as she is mind-gone-far she is safe."

"And if she recovers?"

Ken did not answer. *If they're big enough, they're old enough*, ran through his mind.

"What will you do?"

"I want to run now, Lila. Run as I've never run before. Fight to the second to the last cartridge and then save that for myself."

"Yes," she said. "I know. But will you?"

"You want me to turn myself over to *him?*"

"God no!"

"Then there is no purpose in coming here to see me."

"You know the Apache. Isn't there some way we can deal with them?"

Something unseen was closing in upon him. But why him? Why Ken Driscoll? He had come into the dangerous Bold Butte country to stop the filthy whiskey-running being done by the men who were in the house just below him.

They were to blame for their dealings with an inhuman monster like Loco. For money, for pure greed, with no regard for the consequences as long as they themselves were not forced to pay with their own blood.

"Ken?"

He looked down at her. She was more important to him than any of them, and it was something he could not have foreseen. "You cannot make deals with Loco," he said.

She turned and walked toward the house and he watched her go.

Lila was at the house now. She turned and looked back at him and then she was gone.

Cold realization came to him. If he did not go to Loco, Loco would come to the ranch. Kathy was already his, with or without her mind, but there were other females at Bold Butte Ranch—Amy and Lila Ives and the Mexican girl Dorotea.

There was no sign of life at the house. He padded forward to the west wall and stood up on a rock to look over it. The patio was empty in the bright sunlight. He climbed the wall and dropped silently onto the hard-packed earth. There was a door to his left which led into the west wing of the house. He stepped back into the deep doorway and felt behind him for the door handle. The door opened easily at his touch and he was inside the long hall which led back to the corridor, which in turn led into the living room.

The hallway was still littered with trash. Three of the rooms which opened onto the hallway were used for various stores, while the last room held the piles of kerosene cans.

He walked softly toward the other corridor with his rifle at hip level and the hammer back at full cock. The house was deathly quiet. He stood for a time at the meeting of the two corridors and then walked softly toward the door which led into the large room.

12

IT was cool in the big room for the thick walls kept off the heat of the day. All of the men were there, sitting uneasily with their glasses in their hands, with the exception of the kid, Niles Dunlap, who leaned against the wall near the front door idly paring his nails with his knife.

"Lila swears he won't come," said Jonce quietly.

"I'll send Tequila after him," said Reno.

Jonce spat into the cold fireplace. "Him? He's got a snootful."

"Driscoll won't leave this canyon alive, one way or another," said Reno.

The door leading to the corridor swung fully open. "Maybe you won't either, Reno," said Ken Driscoll as he stepped into the room. "Don't move, Vestel!" he snapped.

"Put down that gun," said Jonce Ives to Ken.

Ken eyed him. He wasn't worried about Ives, for the man obviously wasn't a killer.

"You heard him," said Morg Vestel loudly.

Ken turned a little. "The big he-coon speaks with a voice of brass," he said dryly. "Come and get it, Morg."

Reno wet his full lips. "You came here for a reason, Driscoll, or do you want a fight?"

"Come on out from behind Jonce, Reno. You and that damned 'breed of yours are the only two here I can't get a clean shot at."

Tequila hiccuped. *"Coche!"* he spat at Ken. "Knife and awl to you, you yellow-eyed bastard."

Tequila dropped a hand to his knife.

Ken grinned. "I'm too valuable for you to kill, 'breed. How many notches do you have on that *besh* you carry? Mawson? Vanbrugh? How many others?"

Reno squared his shoulders. "Cut the fight talk, Driscoll."

Jonce nodded. He looked over his shoulder, in the direction of the unseen butte. "Is there anything you can do for her, Driscoll?" he asked.

"I'll talk about it over a drink," he said quietly, "and none of that rotgut slop you've been trading to Loco."

All eyes were on him. "You always did talk too much," said Vestel.

Jonce cut a hand at Reno. "Shut up, you!" He eyed Ken. "You're welcome to a drink. All you like." Jonce looked at the others. "This man is my guest. In my house. Understand?"

Ken rounded the end of the bar and the 'breed spat on Ken's moccasins. The reaction from the lean scout was so swift and deadly that Tequila was lying against the wall spitting blood and teeth from his smashed mouth before any of the others knew what had happened.

Reno looked down at the 'breed and shook his head.

Jonce turned to the big ex-officer. "You keep that 'breed under control, Reno. I don't want Driscoll harmed."

"Is that so? You running things now, Jonce?"

There was no fear in the pale eyes of Jonce Ives. "That's my little niece up there on that butte," he said softly, *"and don't you ever forget it."*

The liquor was good rye, thought Ken, nothing like the swill being imbibed in by Loco and his boys. "What exactly does Loco want, Ives?" he asked.

Jonce emptied his glass. "You," he said flatly.

"Me for the kid, is that it?"

"Yes."

"No more?"

Jonce shook his head.

"You're lying."

Jonce opened his mouth and shut it. He looked at Reno. Reno nodded. "You might as well tell him," he said, "because he'll never be able to tell anyone about it anyway."

Jonce refilled his glass with unsteady hands, slopping liquor on the table. "He wants you, and all the liquor we got."

"Free?"

"Yes."

"Nice deal."

Jonce flushed. "We never had no trouble with him before."

"You damned fool! Do you think you can trust *him*?"

"Reno said it would be all right."

"Reno never did know Apaches." Ken looked at the big officer and then back at Jonce. "How much time do you have?"

Jonce eyed Tequila.

The 'breed wiped blood from his chin and then pointed down the canyon. "When sun is there," he said.

"An hour," said Ken. "What do you aim to do?"

"He wants you and the liquor delivered to the springs."

"Like the morning milk and newspaper."

They all eyed Ken. In a way he held the key to their lives, as well as Kathy's. Maybe Loco would be satisfied with the liquor and Ken Driscoll. If not . . . none of them would leave Bold Butte Canyon except in spirit on their way to hell.

Ken leaned against the wall. "Maybe he'll give back Kathy for the liquor."

Jonce shook his head. "I'll swear to God, Driscoll, he'd rather have you than the liquor, and that's saying a lot."

Niles Dunlap shut his clasp knife with a sharp click. "*Why*, Driscoll?" he asked in a quiet voice.

They all looked at the lean scout but Ken refilled his glass.

The answer came from an unexpected source. Tequila stared with hatred at Ken. "They call him Tats-ah-das-ay-go, the Quick Killer," he said through his broken mouth. "Toga-de-chuz has not forgotten Lost Creek."

"Nor have I, *coche*," said Ken.

132

"You are brave now, Quick Killer. Will you be a woman when the knives and the fire touch your skin?"

Ken whipped out his knife and held it toward the 'breed. "Tell Toga-de-chuz to meet me alone at the springs with his *besh* honed to a razor's edge. He and I will fight it out."

Tequila let an expression pass over his flat face, which might remotely have been a smile. "Why, *coche?*"

"Is he afraid?" Ken snarled.

"Why should he fight when he can have you delivered into his hands as helpless as a baby?"

Jonce wet his lips. "For chrissakes," he said. "Time is running out."

"Let's get the liquor," said Slim nervously.

Federico nodded. He glanced at Ken. "Maybe he'll be satisfied with the liquor."

Reno leaned forward. "Why are you here at Bold Butte, Driscoll?"

"Passing through, Reno."

"You're a damned liar! Things are coming back to me now. Months and months ago they asked you to come back into service as a civilian scout to track down the whiskey runners."

"So?"

133

"I heard about Lost Creek. You dropped out of sight after that. Where did you go?"

They were all watching him now and he knew he'd be shot to doll rags before he got more than one or two of them.

"*Where did you go*, Driscoll?"

There was no answer to give; nothing that he could say would save him now.

Reno turned and looked at the others. "He came here looking for whiskey runners."

Morg Vestel spat. "He found them," he said dryly.

Ken walked to the table and placed his rifle upon it. He drew out his knife and placed it beside the rifle.

"Toga-de-chuz," said Tequila. He laughed.

"Get the liquor," said Jonce to his men.

Morg Vestel walked across the room. He gripped the end of the bar and swung it outward. It moved easily on a silent pivot. Beneath it was a trap door set into the flooring. Morg gripped the ring and raised the door. He lighted a candle and went down a ladder. The others gathered about the trap door and Slim took the first object which was passed up to him by Vestel. It was one of the kerosene cans, the same type as the others Ken had seen.

One by one the cans came up through the opening in Vestel's thick hands until there were about thirty of them stacked near the door.

The door swung open. Federico had brought burros from the corral. With the help of Slim he placed the cans in *aparejos* which had been slung to the burros' backs.

Niles Dunlap glanced at Ken. "Run for it," he said out of the side of his mouth. He drew his Colt partway from its holster, as though to offer it to Ken.

Ken shook his head.

"Outside, you," said Reno to Ken.

He walked out into the bright sunlight. The canyon was quiet. High above the canyon the butte seemed to doze in the sun.

The brave man dies once, the coward many times, thought Ken. But the man who had written those lines had never been in the position Ken was in.

Reno lighted a cigar and puffed it into life. "Morg," he said, "you, Slim, the Kid and Federico take the goods to the spring. Tequila will translate for you."

"No," said Tequila.

"What the hell do you mean by that?" snapped Reno.

"Loco say all come. All men."

"Why?"

Tequila shrugged. "*All* he say."

"What's he up to?" asked Jonce.

Reno took the cigar from his mouth. He looked toward the springs.

"Afraid?" asked Ken dryly.

Jonce wet his lips. "We got to go then," he said.

"Funny, isn't it?" asked Ken as he got up. "You had the whiphand for a time, or *thought* you did. Now he's got you on the run and he won't stop until he bleeds you white. One way or another, Jonce. *One way or another.*"

The women had come out into the yard. Lila's face was white and taut. Dorotea showed her naked fear. Amy laughed. "The big, brave hero," she said. "Loco will see the color of your guts, Driscoll."

"Be quiet," said Lila.

Amy turned. Her wrapper swung open, revealing her sweat-stained negligee. Morg grinned. "Don't talk to your aunt that way, Lila," snapped Amy.

The men eyed the two women, forgetting for the moment the fear which held them.

Maynard Reno held up a big hand. "Let her alone, Lila," he said.

"I've had enough of all of you," Lila spat back. "Call yourselves *men?* Sheep have more guts than all of you except Ken Driscoll." She stood glaring at Reno.

The sweat ran down their faces as they stood there. Reno shook his head. "Time's almost gone, Jonce."

They all looked at Ken. Lila walked to him and kissed him. "I'll try to save you," she whispered.

They walked toward the springs, leaving her behind.

High up on the slopes of the butte a pair of liquid eyes had been watching the scene in the courtyard.

"Damn them! Where are they?" It was Jonce Ives who spoke. He mopped his wet face and looked toward the butte trail.

They had been waiting for the better part of an hour and the heat was hellish in the canyon while a shimmering haze rose from the baking rock of the butte.

The kerosene cans were piled beside the springs. The men sat in the hot shade of the trees, smoking and always looking toward the butte trail, but it seemed that all life had vanished from the butte.

"Maybe they won't come," said Slim hopefully.

Morg spat. "You get stupider every day, Slim."

Niles Dunlap whittled at a stick with a long-bladed bowie knife and now and then he glanced at Ken Driscoll who squatted beside a boulder with his long arms dangling over his knees, seemingly oblivious to heat and danger.

Tequila stood up, wiped his face and walked toward the pile of cans. He picked up one of them and began to work at its top.

"What the hell!" said Jonce.

"Let him alone!" warned Reno.

The 'breed had the lid loose now and he poured the liquid on the ground. The reek of kerosene came to Ken. Tequila thrust a dirty hand into the can and withdrew another can. He threw the kerosene can aside and squatted in the sunlight, prying off the lid of the second can with his knife. When the lid clattered on the ground he raised the can and began to drink.

"Pretty clever, eh, Driscoll?" asked Reno.

Ken nodded. No one would think of carrying

liquor inside a kerosene can other than men like Reno and Ives, and such innocent merchandise would never be suspect.

Tequila swayed back and forth until finally the can was empty. He hurled it into the clean waters of the spring.

"Jesus," said Slim.

The 'breed felt for his knife, drew it and began to walk toward Ken. "*Coche*," he said. The thin veneer of civilization had been stripped from him by the liquor.

Reno laughed. "Let him wait for Loco, Tequila," he said.

"Won't have to wait long," said Morg Vestel. "Here they come."

A line of warriors had appeared on the butte trail, jogging along with their kilts flapping about their muscular legs. They stopped on the rock ledge just above the springs and looked down at the men who stood there waiting for them.

"Loco ain't there," said Jonce out of the side of his mouth.

A squat warrior stepped forward and looked down at them. "It is good," he said in his own tongue. He eyed Ken. "Tats-ah-das-ay-go. We meet again."

Ken nodded. It was Na-da-hi-ate, a minor chief of the Tontos and a good warrior. He had been at Lost Creek.

"Toga-de-chuz is waiting for you," said the Apache.

"Where is the *day-den?*"

"She will be sent down when you are up there."

"So?"

"I do not lie, Quick Killer."

"Let's get this over with," said Reno nervously.

The Apaches came down to the springs and began to pick up the heavy cans. Na-da-hi-ate grunted in satisfaction. *"Schlanh. Schlango,"* he said.

"Where's the kid?" demanded Jonce.

"She'll be down when I get up there."

"You sure?"

Ken shrugged. *"Quien sabe?* Who's sure of *anything* now?"

The warriors started back up the trail and when they were a good hundred yards away, the sub-chief turned to Ken. "Come," he said.

Ken walked forward. The warrior drew a heavy Starr revolver from his waist band and jerked it toward the trail. Ken walked forward with cold sweat running from his armpits. He did not look back.

They had reached the foot of the trail when the first scream was heard by them, echoing through the canyon from the ranch.

Ken turned his head but the muzzle of the revolver jabbed against his kidneys.

Another scream tore the quietness into shreds.

"The women!" yelled Jonce.

Ken turned, flinging up his left arm and catching the Apache across the bridge of his broad nose with the elbow, while he drove down his right hand to grip the Starr and turn it aside. It exploded under his grip and the slug smashed into the ground. Ken smashed a knee up into the Apache's groin and as he doubled forward in pain the other knee met his down-coming face. Ken jerked the Starr from the nerveless grasp of the warrior and brought it down with killing force atop the thick mane of hair. The brave fell backward from the ledge and struck the hard rock bottom of the first pool. He lay still.

The men were running for the ranch now, with the exception of Tequila, who stood there stupidly with his knife in his hand.

Ken ran down the trail. Tequila tried to focus his eyes and as he saw Ken he drew back his arm for a cast of the knife but the big Starr bucked twice in Ken's hand and the heavy slugs ripped into Tequila's chest. He went down and Ken hurdled him as he raced after the others towards the ranch.

The six men were well in the lead, with Jonce at their head and Slim close behind him when the gunfire broke out from the side of the canyon like the ripping of heavy cloth. Slim staggered sideways as half a dozen slugs chewed into his gangling body. Federico cursed as a bullet skinned his left shoulder, while Morg Vestel hit the ground when a heel was torn from one of his boots. The men scattered into cover, leaving Slim lying there with the red blood turning black as it soaked into the thirsty earth.

Ken dived into cover and raised the big Starr but there was nothing to shoot at. Smoke drifted down the canyon but there was nothing to see. Minutes ticked past and then high on the slopes, where the trail began, a figure moved. It was Loco. He stood up and looked down into the canyon. He began his weird laughter, then turned and motioned with his hand. Two of his bucks came forward and each of them held a woman by the wrists. Their hair fell over their faces, and one of them had golden hair while the other had thick chestnut hair.

Ken's blood seemed to chill. Loco had pulled another one of his tricks. No wonder he had not come to the springs. He had gone to the unprotected ranch house and taken the women. But where was Dorotea?

The people on the slopes vanished as suddenly as they had appeared. Ken stood up. He walked toward the others.

"Get down, you fool!" yelled the kid.

Ken stopped and looked down at them. "You can't make deals with Loco," he said thinly.

They found Dorotea lying in the littered kitchen. She had been stripped and her neck was bent awkwardly. Her dark eyes were wide open but the glaze of death had dulled them. She lay atop the great stove and they had started a roaring fire in it. The stench of burning flesh hung heavily in the hot room.

Ken pulled the slim body from the stove and swathed it in a rug. He carried her into Amy's room, placed her on the bed and then shut the door behind him.

Everything of value and many things of no value had been stripped from the ranch house.

Flour, salt, molasses and tea lay intermingled in the kitchen. Urine stunk in most of the rooms where the drunken bucks had relieved themselves.

An unseen presence had moved into the room. The men were silenced by crushing fear.

13

A SINGLE candle guttered in the neck of a bottle on the zinc-topped bar, casting alternate patches of light on the smoke-colored beams, or plunging them into darkness.

Jonce sat with his elbows on the table and his head between his hands. "Jesus, oh Jesus," he said hoarsely.

Federico crossed himself. He had said little since they had found Dorotea. "It would be better if they were dead," he said.

Ken poured a drink and looked at the amber fluid. The liquor had no effect upon him.

The kid came into the room from outside. "You can see lights up there now," he said quietly.

"With plenty of liquor and two white women," said Morg.

"Shut up!" snapped the kid.

Vestel spat. "You want I should hold a wake?"

"Driscoll," pleaded the kid.

145

Ken downed his drink. "Loco has maybe forty or fifty warriors up there. Plenty of guns and ammunition. Every yard of that trail up the butte would be like walking into the waiting room of hell."

Jonce nodded hopelessly. "I went partway up that trail once," he said, "whilst hunting deer. Got halfway to the top and sprained my ankle. Didn't fall or nothing, just suddenly sat down with a sprained ankle."

"Bull crap," said Vestel.

Federico drummed on the table with his fingers. "Six of us could not get up that trail, nor could sixty."

"Six *hundred*," said Ken dryly.

"It's their fort," said Reno, "as much of a citadel as was ever built by any white man."

"There's one long shot left," he said.

"The hero speaks," sneered Vestel.

"What is it, Driscoll?" asked Jonce. His voice shook.

Ken jerked a thumb over his shoulder. "Climb the west side of the butte."

The whites of their eyes showed but none of them spoke. Ken leaned back against the wall and rolled a cigarette. He lighted it and eyed them through the smoke. "Well?"

"You're loco," said Vestel.

"It cannot be done," said Federico.

"Hopeless," said Jonce.

"Damned fool to think of it," sneered Reno.

"I'll go, Driscoll, but you'll have to lead the way."

Jonce wet his lips. "She was a whore," he said softly, "but dammit, she was good to me for awhile . . ."

Federico shrugged. "We are only on this accursed earth a short time. Perhaps, in time to come, people will speak of Federico Rafael Zaldivar as *muy hombre!*"

"To hell with it!" snapped Vestel.

"No guts," said the kid.

Vestel stood up. "I'll go anywhere any man in this room will go!"

"Then shut up!" said the kid. "Put your feet where your mouth is!"

Reno wet his lips. "I'll make a deal," he said.

"Figures," said Ken. He poured a drink.

"I'll go. If we get down safe you keep your mouth shut about the whiskey-running."

Ken nodded. "Provided you get out of this country pronto!"

"Agreed!"

147

The man was a liar. There was no telling what his game was.

"What do we do?" asked Jonce.

"Get out of here and up the first slopes before the moon rises," said Ken. "If we're caught on those slopes in the moonlight we'll look like insect specimens pinned to cardboard. We'll need water, slings for the rifles, ropes and riatas. Get moving!"

When they were ready they gathered for a final drink. "Supposing they're out there waiting for us?" asked Jonce nervously.

Ken spat. "They've got other things on their heathen minds."

Ken was the first out. He padded across the dark courtyard and scaled the wall. They followed him one by one. They walked quickly toward the brush beneath the first slope.

Ken threaded his way through a jungle of rocks and brush, stippled with cholla and catclaw which struck and clung to clothing and flesh alike.

When he reached the base of the first great bastion of rock he looked back and waited for the others. To the south there was nothing to see but a pool of darkness, and far beyond that the darker pool of the empty desert and he

148

wished to God he was out in that pool of darkness.

Rock clattered and the kid appeared, wiping the sweat from his face. "And this is only the beginning," he said.

"Have a drink."

"I don't drink."

"You will before *this* night is over, kid."

Ken went on when the others had caught up with him. It would be by guess and by God, and if moonlight found them stranded on a naked ridge it would be all over. And, if they did make it, what then? Six exhausted white men up against half a hundred liquored-up savages.

The sweat broke out on them as they plowed through the shintangle. There was a faint trace of moonlight coming from the southern shoulder of the butte when Ken finally reached the foot of the long, knife-edged ridge which slanted transversely up into the darkness. He dropped to the ground and felt the warm rush of sweat break out on him and the damned, intolerable itching which came with it.

He could hear them scrabbling for footholds on the naked rock and then one by one they dropped down near him. "Drink?" asked Ken of the kid.

"No."

"Madre de Diablo," groaned Federico.

"This is only the first floor," said the kid with a grin.

Jonce looked up at the dark towering mass above them. "We can't make it, Driscoll."

"Go back then!"

Vestel shifted his chew and then spat. "You aim to go up that razor-edge behind you?"

"You know another way?"

Ken got up and started the climb.

"Let us rest!" said Jonce.

Ken ignored them. He shifted the rope coils to his left shoulder. The kid followed him.

"Mary had a little lamb," said Vestel.

They got up and followed the kid.

The moon tinted the sky and far below them they could see the deep trench of the shadowed canyon. The ridge fell away from them, almost vertically, and to the south of them it seemed to taper off to a weather-honed edge of paper thickness.

None of them looked behind them and up at the great mass of the butte which had now

150

begun to take on the shape by which it was recognized for fifty miles in every direction. They had hardly challenged the butte itself as yet. It was waiting for the trial of strength, but before that it would wear them down, little by little. It could wait.

Ken began to work his way up the ridge. A fragment of rock broke loose under one foot and it seemed like a long, long time before it struck far below them.

Then the ledge petered out and his questing hands met nothing but air. He lay flat on his belly and probed the darkness with his eyes. There was a sheer drop of hundreds of feet below him. To his left was a gap but he had no idea how deep it was. Ten feet or less, across the gap, was another transverse ledge, trending on up into the further darkness.

"What's up?" husked the kid behind Ken.

"The butte," said Ken dryly.

"Funny man!"

Ken looked back over his shoulder. "Can you fly, kid?"

"Not too well."

"You might have to."

The kid craned his neck like a turtle to look at the gap. "Yeh," he said softly.

Ken took a line and made a noose in it. He straddled the ridge and cast the line over his head and toward the far ledge. It struck and dropped. His third try was a success. He drew the line taut and tested it.

"Hand over hand?" asked the kid.

Ken turned to face the gap, legs dangling, drew in the line tight, then slid from the edge with a muttered prayer on his dry lips. He plunged from sight and then his feet struck the far side and he scrambled quickly up the rope to crawl over the edge and lie still with the sweat of fear and exertion draining from his tired body.

"Hey," called the kid. "You hit bottom yet?"

"You little bastard!" Ken sat up, coiled the line and hurled it back. "Catch!"

The kid caught the line, gripped it, let his legs drop and hit just below Ken before he realized what had happened. Ken gave him a hand up. "Next!" called out the kid.

The four men straddled the ridge. Ken could make out their faces. Federico was first. Ken tested the line for cuts or worn spots, then coiled it and tossed it across to the Mexican. He crossed himself and then swung easily across to them and they hauled him up.

Reno made the passage safely and then Morg Vestel flew across like a great ungainly bird, cursing as he smashed against the rock. Ken coiled the line and looked across at Jonce. The rancher made no effort to catch the line. Instead he drew out a bottle and up-ended it. "Catch, damn you!" said Ken.

Jonce lowered the bottle. "How do we get back?"

The five of them looked at each other. There *was* no way back. It was up the butte or nothing.

"Catch!" called Ken.

Jonce worked his way down the ridge.

"Yellowbelly!" said Reno.

Jonce stopped. "She's only a whore," he said.

"What about Lila and Kathy?" asked the kid.

"They're dead by now."

Ives stood up. He drained his bottle and looked down the long dangerous incline. He swayed and then went over the edge. A dull thud came to the men on the ledge, then a harsh dry rattling of stones, followed closely by the splintering crash of the bottle far below. Then the echoes slowly died away down the canyon and it was as silent as it had been before Jonce Ives fell to his death.

Ken Driscoll stood up and wiped the sweat from his face. "Come on," he said. "The moon will be up soon."

They followed him up the ledge.

The moon was to the southwest of the butte and its light silvered the top of the great monolith but there were still deep shadows on the western face. Ken had worked his way up a chimney cleft by bracing hands and feet against one side and his back against the other.

One by one they followed him to the top. Beyond and above them the butte formed a great series of natural steps, a little over the height of a tall man, which must be ascended before they could reach the last great height of the butte.

Federico looked at the butte top. "It will take flies to scale that," he said.

"Scairt, Mex?" asked Vestel.

"Damn you! I will show you!"

The Mexican jumped to his feet and attacked the first step, a rotting, crumbling mess. He scaled it easily and looked back as he reached up for the next one. "I will show you who will be first in the attack!"

He pulled himself up and something moved on a level with his face. There was a lightning swift movement of a flat ugly head and it struck hard against Federico's face. He fell backward and the rattlesnake moved off with an angry buzzing.

The kid ran to Federico and turned him over where he lay. "Jesus," said Niles softly.

The fang marks were just below the left eye. Ken let his hand drop from his knife. There was no chance now to bleed the man. Niles reached down quickly and jerked the Mexican's pistol from its holster. Ken eyed the kid. There was no chance to save Federico and there could be no shooting until they went into the attack.

Federico slowly touched his face. It was stiff from the smashing blow and the venom was already working within him. How long could a man live this way? He looked up at the others. He held out a shaking hand. *"Mi pistola,"* he pleaded.

They did not speak.

"Dios en cielo!" The eyes were wide. "Then kill me!"

"You have your knife," said the kid quietly.

"Madre de Dios! Do not leave me here alone!"

Ken swung up the rise and did not look back. One after the other they came after him, leaving Federico Rafael Zaldivar to meet his god alone.

They were almost there. The moonlight bathed them as they fought their way up the last precipitous incline. From far below the upper part of the butte had always looked glass-smooth, streaked by fine, hairlike striations, but they weren't striations; they were deep cracks and crevices wrought into the tough granite by the forces of wind, frost and rain.

"Listen!" said the kid.

They were clinging to a bald rock face which seemed to bulge out, ready to drop them hundreds of feet if they made a slip.

A faint, throbbing noise came to them.

"They're praying to the moon," said Ken.

"You loco?" demanded Vestel.

Ken turned his head. The moon had passed the butte and was now bathing the entire western face in cold silvery light. *"Gun-ju-le, Klego-na-ay,"* he said. *"Ek!"*

"What did you say in Apache?" asked Niles.

"Be good, oh Moon. For luck, kid, for luck."

"Look up there!" snapped Reno.

They craned their necks. A woman stood at

156

the edge of the cliff in the full moonlight. She looked down and then back over her shoulder. The moonlight glistened on her long fine golden hair and her naked body. She hesitated, looked straight out into space and then stepped over the edge as though entering a pool. She shot past the four white-faced men clinging to the cliff.

"Good God," said Vestel hoarsely. "That was Amy Ives!"

"Quiet!" snapped Ken. "Look!"

Four men had appeared on the edge of the cliff as though materialized from moonbeams by an Apache *diyi*. They looked down for a moment and then they vanished as quickly as they had appeared.

Vestel fumbled for his bottle, lost his grip on it and cursed as it skidded down the rock face and shot off into space. He cursed again as they heard the brittle crash far below.

Ken closed his eyes. He remembered the well-shaped body of Amy Ives, the great blue eyes, the golden hair and the creamy white flesh.

The last obstacle was just above them; the craggy lip of the butte. The drum-throbbing came through the night. Morgan Vestel wet his thick lips and stared with fear-haunted eyes at the cliff edge. The chips were down now.

"Up we go," said Ken.

"With half a hundred 'Paches against us?" demanded Vestel. "You loco?"

"I knew he'd yellow out," said the kid. "The he-coon."

"I ain't afraid," said the big man, but the stench of fear rose from his body.

"Come on then," jeered the kid.

Vestel slid a little lower. "It's too steep," he mouthed. He slid a little further down the slope like a great ungainly crab until only his face and hat showed to the others. Suddenly he stood up on a narrow ledge and then began to run down the steep incline. He gained speed and tried to stop but it was no use. Faster and faster until he stepped out into sheer space, seemed to tread the air, then dropped from sight to strike far below and as he hit there was a splintering of glass beneath him. The bottle which had given him the false courage to ascend Bold Butte was with him at the end.

Ken slid over the edge and lay still. The others crouched just below the rim. The terrain was a mess. Shattered and splintered rock littered an area in a hell's kitchen of confusion.

Interspersed and interlaced through the masses of loose rock was a mat of thorny brush.

The thudding of the drums came to him and the bitter-sweet odor of woodsmoke. He bellied forward, thrusting his Winchester ahead of him.

The butte was cup-shaped here, although probably Ken was the first white man to discover that fact. A great natural fortress with deep granite holes which probably held water a good part of the year. A man could live up there a long time, safe from attack, watching the one trail which led up to his domain.

God alone knew how long the Apaches had used this place. No one had ever challenged them there.

The drums thudded on and on. Ken whistled softly. His two companions came up over the edge and Ken almost grinned at the incongruity of it all. A wet-nosed kid and two bitter enemies challenging the might of Bold Butte and of Loco, the invincible.

"Stay here," whispered Ken.

He worked his way through the maze until he could see the fires and the camp. Warriors staggered about, dancing and falling, swilling liquor from cans. A wickiup stood beneath a tip-tilted slab of rock. A young Apache stood before it. There was a woman sitting just inside the door of the wickiup. Ken could not see her face but he knew it must be Lila.

Loco staggered into the firelight and waved a drinking olla. Sweat ran down his face and mingled with his paint. Then a little figure appeared, wandering into the firelight, close to the drunken chief.

"Kathy!" said the kid.

Ken cut a hand at him to be quiet.

"Patsy," said the little girl.

She wandered out of the firelight and toward the wickiup. The brave touched the fetishes at his neck but she passed him and wandered into the rock maze. Ken's hands closed on her dress and he wormed his way back with the little girl.

The kid took her from Ken. Ken looked up. The brave had wandered over toward the rocks looking for Kathy. He was close to Niles. The little girl squirmed and the Apache bent close over a rock. The kid had his knife out and into the Apache before he knew what had hit him.

The kid's face was greasy white as he came back to Ken.

"Your first?" asked Ken.

"Yes."

"Want that drink now?"

"Hell, yes!"

Ken looked about as the kid drank. "Where's Reno?"

"Damned if I know."

Ken bellied forward. Lila had crawled from the wickiup and was looking about. Then she came swiftly toward the rocks. Ken whistled softly and she stopped. "Come on!" he hissed. They might not save her life but they at least could save her from what would come if the Apaches had her alive.

She stared into the rock clutter with a puzzled look on her face. "Ken?"

"Yes, dammit! Get in here!"

She came to him and his strong arms drew her close as though he would crush her. "Kathy?" she gasped.

"With Niles."

"Thank God!"

He looked up. "We're not through yet," he said quietly.

The drumming suddenly stopped.

Ken shoved her back behind a boulder. He gripped his Winchester and stood up. There was no use in hiding now. They would find him in any case.

They stared at him. He was an apparition

engendered from moonbeams and rotgut whiskey, for how could a white man of flesh and blood get to the top of Na-u-kuzze, the Great Bear?

Thick silence hung over the butte top. Then slowly the warriors farthest from the fires began to back toward the twisted, tortuous trail by which they gained and left their stronghold. There was no other way to reach the butte top, but the white man was there, and how had he come? Perhaps he was a wandering spirit from Chidin-bi-Kungua, The House of Spirits.

An owl hooted softly. That was enough for the Apaches. Bu was the omen of evil. There was a soft rushing of moccasined feet on the trail and they were gone, all but one, who stood in the light of the fires, staring fixedly at Ken. It was Loco, Toga-de-chuz, the madman; the sly raider and bloody murderer.

The fire crackled. There was a soft moaning of wind.

Loco hurled his olla into the fire and drew his knife, holding it issuing from the thumb side of his hand, as used in butchering an animal, not in meeting a man. It was an insult which would cut an Apache's pride more than steel would hurt his flesh.

162

Ken leaned his rifle against a rock. He strode forward, feeling for his knife, and his questing fingers met the empty sheath. It was too late. Loco charged and the blade flicked out, tracing a red course down Ken's outthrust left arm. There was sure victory in Loco's eyes. *"Ahagahe!"* he snarled.

The blade drew blood from Ken's shoulder and then was feinted toward his groin. *"Zastee! Zastee!"* snarled Loco. *"Kill! Kill!"*

Ken staggered back, feigning fear and panic. Loco closed in swiftly and lithely, with extended blade. But the liquor was false to him and he forgot natural Apache caution. Ken stepped to his left, gripped Loco's knife wrist and dragged hard at it while at the same time he thrust his right leg in front of the chief. Loco went down hard.

Ken ripped the reddened knife from Loco's nerveless grasp and sank it beneath the left ribs. *"Yah-tats-an!"* he said, as though he was giving an animal its death blow. He twisted the blade viciously.

It seemed as though he was now alone on the butte. There was one thing he must do at once. He bent over the dead chief and worked swiftly and when he stood up he held the head of Loco

163

by its long thick hair. He picked up a branch and carried it to the head of the trail where he forced it into a cleft. He sharpened the upper end and drove the head firmly on to it, with the sightless eyes staring down the trail.

Loco had led his warriors well in life; now he would drive them away in death.

14

HE found the kid lying amongst the rocks, face downward. There was a cold feeling within him as he turned Niles over. But the kid was only unconscious.

"Leave your rifle there," said the voice behind Ken.

Ken turned to look at Maynard Reno. The ex-officer held a cocked Colt in his hand. "Where are they?" asked Ken.

"I told them to hide."

Ken eyed the big man. He had never trusted him.

"Walk toward the cliff, Driscoll."

Ken walked toward the brink. "Nice deal for you, Reno," he said over his shoulder.

Reno laughed. "You didn't think I was going to let you live, did you?"

"I thought you might have gained a conscience."

"Bull crap!"

Ken could see far across the western country, silvered by the bright moonlight. Far below him was the canyon and the ranch, looking like a handful of children's blocks.

"What about the others?" asked Ken quietly.

"The kid will follow you to hell, Driscoll."

"And the woman and child?"

"They don't know anything about this. I can say you both died fighting. Make a hero out of you, Driscoll. You'll be the dead hero and I'll be the live one. Maynard Reno, the hero who led the impossible attack on Bold Butte, killed Loco and saved the two sisters. Neat, eh?"

Ken nodded. It was neat . . . for Reno.

"Turn around."

Ken turned. Reno was a foot away from him with his Colt at belt level. "I want to see your face when you go over," said Reno. He grinned. "Lila isn't a bad looking woman," he said. "She owns Bold Butte Ranch now. I can be quite gallant, Driscoll. A few months for her to mourn and then move in. The squire of Bold Butte, eh?"

"Ken!" yelled the kid.

The Colt came past Reno, end over end and the butt smacked into Ken's calloused palm. His left hand swept back the hammer as he fanned three shots at pointblank range into Reno's belly.

Reno staggered, dropped his gun, opened his mouth to let out a flood of blood, then stepped cleanly from the edge of the precipice as the echoes died away one by one.

The kid came slowly toward Ken. "He buffaloed me, Ken, when I wasn't looking."

"That's the best way to do it," said Ken dryly. "Thanks, kid."

"Let's get the girls," said the kid.

Ken took out his flask and passed it to the kid. He drank deeply, then passed it back to Ken. Ken drained most of it, leaving a good slug in it. He held it up to the light, then tossed the glass flask over the edge. "Jesus!" said the kid. "There was a drink still in it."

Ken grinned. "The butte has to have a drink too, kid. A libation to the gods, as it were."

THE END

Other titles in the
Linford Western Library:

TOP HAND
by Wade Everett

The Broken T was big enough for a man on the run to hire out as a cowhand and be safe. But no ranch is big enough to let a man hide from himself.

GUN WOLVES OF LOBO BASIN
by Lee Floren

The Feud was a blood debt. When Smoke Talbot found the outlaws who gunned down his folks he aimed to nail their hide to the barn door.

SHOTGUN SHARKEY
by Marshall Grover

The westbound coach carrying the indomitable Larry and Stretch and their mixed bag of allies headed for a shooting showdown.